ALMOS[illegible]

ALMOST LIKE SPRING

A Novel

ALEX CAPUS

Translated by
John Brownjohn

First published in German as *Fast ein bißchen Früling* in 2002

First published in English in 2013 by
HAUS PUBLISHING LTD.
70 Cadogan Place, London SW1X 9AH
www.hauspublishing.com

Print ISBN 978 1 908323 33 0
ebook ISBN 978 1 908323 34 7

Typeset in Garamond by MacGuru Ltd
info@macguru.org.uk

Printed in the United Kingdom

A CIP catalogue for this book is available from the British Library

1

This is the true story of Kurt Sandweg and Waldemar Velte, two bank robbers who set off for India from Wuppertal in the winter of 1933/34, intending to travel there by sea. They only got as far as Basel, where they fell in love with a shop assistant who sold gramophone records and bought a tango disc from her every day. My maternal grandmother went for a walk with the bank robbers on two occasions. A police squad almost shot my grandfather in open countryside because he vaguely resembled one of them.

❧

Situated in Basel's Marktplatz is Globus, a department store with a splendid Art Nouveau façade. It is lunchtime on 13 December 1933. The female shop assistants are sitting at the rough pine tables in the staff refreshment room on the top floor, eating sandwiches they've brought from home. Seated to the fore are members of the permanent staff in white skirts; the temporary shop assistants wear blue skirts and sit at the table right at the back. Today, as usual, they're spending every minute of their lunch break bickering.

'Guess who the management have chosen to be Fräulein Friendly this week? Olga Vollmeier!'

'What?! The Vollmeier girl? Potato Face, you mean?'
'The one with the nose like a parrot?'
'And hair like a monkey?'
'You mean *she's* going to be Fräulein Friendly?'
'I heard she goes to the pictures with the head of advertising.'
'The head of department!'
'The head of advertising!'
'The head of department!'
'Fräulein Friendly, pfft! Standing around in Marktplatz till Christmas in that stupid get-up, shaking a thousand children's sticky hands and doling out nuts and gingerbread – who'd want to do that?'
'You do get a bonus.'
'But if you have to earn it by going to the pictures with the head of advertising!'
'*You'd* go like a shot.'
'What, me?'
'With the head of department!'
'The head of advertising!'
'The pictures or anywhere else, for that matter!'
'Like where?'
'Speaking for myself –'
'Did you hear? At the Rheinbrücke Department Store they flew in Santa Claus in a biplane!'
'Who would *you* choose to be Fräulein Friendly?'
'Men are scared of you.'
'They aren't scared of *you,* that's common knowledge.'
'Hey, if you don't stop it this instant –'
'Come on, who would *you* choose?'
'I'd vote for … Dorly!'
Cheers.

'Dorly! Dorly! You're our Fräulein Friendly!'

A tall young woman with short, dark hair has been listening to this argument in silence. The girls on either side fling their arms round her. Dorly Schupp uses her elbows to repel these spurious caresses. She pulls a face and glances angrily across the table at the pig-tailed blonde who is watching the scene with her lower lip jutting derisively, for it was she who started the argument and she, too, who brought up Dorly's name – deliberately so, because she had been put on the defensive and needed to get out of the line of fire. Her calculations paid off.

'Stop it! Leave me alone!' Dorly extricates herself from the girls' embrace and gets to her feet. In the commotion, some of the other girls stand up too. Dorly is half a head taller than the rest, as well as slimmer and stronger; if it came to a fight, she would probably take them all on at the same time. 'She was a regular Amazon,' my grandmother used to say in later years. 'She could have throttled a panther with her bare hands.'

Dorly smooths her hair down and straightens her white collar. 'I must go,' she says. 'I'm on lunchtime duty.' She goes downstairs to the record department to relieve her superior, the senior assistant. There are few customers at this hour. Dorly puts a tango on and dusts some shelves. Still hot and bothered after being manhandled and talked at by the others, she relishes the solitude. This never-ending gossip! A fracas has to break out every lunchtime, and then they all get angry – each angrier than the next. It's a regular competition, because your degree of indignation is regarded as a measure of your own righteousness. The angrier you get, the more respectable you are.

A bell pings and the red lift door opens. Customers. Dorly turns, feather duster in hand. Two young men. Well-dressed young men in knickerbockers and expensive tweed overcoats, their hair slicked back. The gramophone is still playing a tango. The newcomers are young and bizarre-looking. They definitely aren't locals. Dorly can recognise locals at a glance – quite how, she couldn't have said; they simply look familiar even if you've never seen them before. These two, by contrast, are probably foreigners. The tall one looks friendly – like an Austrian, say – and the short one could well be a Finn, to judge by his grim expression.

Dorly has to pass the boys to get behind the counter. The gramophone is still playing a tango. The taller of the two, the Austrian, bows and strikes a dancer's pose, and because he's smiling in such a boyishly awkward way, Dorly accepts his invitation for fun and dances a few steps with him in *alla breve* time. She has placed her right hand, plus feather duster, in the Austrian's left, so the tuft of pink feathers dances ahead of them like an inebriated bird. Dorly hopes the head of department doesn't look in. She holds the Austrian away from her and hisses brusque instructions. 'Back straight! Don't look at your feet! Keep your hands up!' The Austrian is a very bad dancer but he obeys, performs some clumsy steps and turns and winks at his little friend, the Finn. The latter, leaning against a concrete column, is watching with his hands buried in his overcoat pockets. The tango ends at last, the needle rasps around the blank groove.

Dorly goes back behind the counter, stows the feather duster somewhere, and straightens her skirt. The tall boy thanks her politely. She notices from his accent that he's German, not Austrian, and probably from the north. Out of the corner of her eye she sees the shorter boy leave the concrete column and come towards her. He's odd. The tall boy is odd enough, but the short one is far more so. Dorly is suddenly very busy tidying her wrapping paper, scissors and gold string.

'They were two very contrasting characters,' Dorly Schupp is reported to have testified five weeks later, when questioned at two in the morning by Basel's district attorney. 'Kurt Sandweg was a boyish daredevil who laughed a lot and could talk the hind legs off a donkey. Waldemar Velte was a serious type who only opened his mouth when he had something to say. I took to both of them from the outset, but especially to Velte, just because he wasn't a charmer.'

The short young man stands in front of the counter and waits for Dorly to look at him. He's not much taller than she is, maybe even a little shorter, taking his rather built-up heels into account.

'Please, Fräulein, I'd like to buy a record.'

'Yes?'

'*In Deine Hände* with Willi Kollo.'

'I'm sorry, I don't know it.'

'It's only just out.'

'I don't believe we have it in stock. One moment, please … No, I'm sorry. I'd have to order it in, then you could pick it up tomorrow.'

'That's no good.' The short boy removes his hands from the counter and turns to go. 'Kurt, what time does our train leave tomorrow morning?'

'Seven forty-eight.'

'We don't open until eight. I'm sorry.'

'So am I. Goodbye, Fräulein.'

'Goodbye.'

Dorly is just turning away when the tall boy catches his friend by the elbow. 'Hey, we could stay on in Basel a day longer if you – well, want to wait for the record. There'll be another train the day after tomorrow.'

'If you say so.'

'Will you be here tomorrow, Fräulein?' asks the tall boy.

'I don't know. I may have to help out in another department.'

'May we know your name?'

Dorly hesitates.

'Shouldn't we be able to say who took our order?'

'No, not really.' Dorly looks over at the short boy. He has turned away as if merely waiting for the lift. 'Well, all right. My name is Viktoria Schupp. My workmates call me Dorly.'

'What's your star sign?'

'*That* you've certainly no need to know!'

'Us two are both Leos. We were born on 3 and 4 August 1910.'

'Only one day apart?'

'I'm the older of us, he's the younger.'

'I'm an Aquarius,' says Dorly. 'February 2, 1908.'

Dorly is lying. She's 32 years old, not 25, and has been divorced for six years. Not that she has ever told anyone at Globus apart from the blonde farmer's daughter named Maria Stifter, who always sits opposite her during their lunch break, and with whom she has become quite friendly.

❧

The two of them lost touch soon afterwards, so my grandmother didn't feel obliged to remain silent in later years. 'Two years of marriage were enough to put her off men for good,' she told me over her shoulder while snipping away at the climbing roses on the veranda. Grandfather, poring over a crossword puzzle at the garden table, irritably clicked his jaw and pretended not to be listening. Grandmother spoke louder than necessary, never once glancing in his direction. 'That Dorly! She didn't shilly-shally – *snip!* – no, she got divorced. *Snip!* Me, I'd never have had the nerve, being just a silly country girl. *Snip!* Mind you, we weren't married yet, your grandfather and I, at the end of '33. Not even properly engaged, for that matter …' At that point, Grandfather pushed his chair back and fled into the house. Grandmother became monosyllabic once he was out of earshot, and a little later she shooed me away with the secateurs.

❧

Dorly Schupp's husband, Anton Beck by name, was a tax inspector and racing cyclist. Although barely 30, he was already cold, formal and introverted in manner, with lean limbs, a hard mouth, and the beginnings of a bald patch at the back of his head. If anyone had asked Dorly what had once attracted her to him, she wouldn't have known what answer to give.

The couple led a well-regulated married life. Dorly had quickly and easily become accustomed to it, having then been young, adaptable and ready to do all the right things. Every Monday night they went to the civil servants' skittle club, where she soon outplayed her husband; Monday was wash day, Friday fish day. On Sundays Dorly went to the cycle races and cheered her Toni on. On one occasion he nearly won the Swiss championship.

All would have been well, had Toni not been afflicted with headaches and backaches whenever the light went out in their bedroom. Dorly had been surprised by this during their first few weeks of marriage, but then she found she could manage quite well without that business. After all, it wasn't a life-threatening deficiency, like starvation or hypothermia. If only Anton hadn't been so unhappy about his incapacity! If only he hadn't kept waking up with a horrified cry whenever he dreamt the curious things he dreamt about; if only he hadn't kept trying to force himself on Dorly with all the strength and stamina of a trained racing cyclist; if only he hadn't been so desperate after each new defeat, and if only he hadn't, in his despair, flown into such a rage that he beat Dorly black and blue and clamped the pillow over her face so the neighbours wouldn't hear her screams. And if only he hadn't been so cringingly hangdog the next morning that any woman was bound to lose all respect for him, and if only the whole process hadn't started all over again three weeks later. At three o'clock one morning, after Toni had once more throttled her until everything went black before her eyes, Dorly packed her bags, walked all the way across the city, and went home to her mother, who occupied a respectable four-roomed apartment and had been living alone since her husband's death. She moved back into her old room, got a shop assistant's job at Globus, and shunned male company from then on.

❧

From the records of Basel CID:

'Waldemar Velte, born 4 August 1910, looks 28–30, unmarried, engineer, German national. Personal description: height 172cm, slim to medium build, fair curly hair combed back, forehead high and retreating, eyes grey-green, nose straight, clean-shaven, upper lip thin, teeth white and well preserved, chin small and rounded. Dimples, longish face, slightly prominent cheekbones. Speaks standard German with a Cologne accent. Clothing: dark grey verging on black. Overcoat, unbelted. Brown suit, coloured sports shirt with collar, dark green felt hat with black ribbon, brim turned down in front, reddish-brown shoes.

'Kurt Sandweg, born 3 August 1910, looks 25–27, unmarried, engineer, German national. Personal description: height 185cm, very slim build, thin, brown hair medium length, parted on left, normal forehead, dark eyes, unremarkable nose, trimmed moustache, rather pouting lips, teeth white and well preserved, chin ordinary, face longish, pale, thin, rather hollow cheeks, pronounced creases around mouth. Friendly expression, speaks standard German with a Cologne accent. Clothing: double-breasted dark grey overcoat belted at back, dark grey pinstripe suit, clothes in good condition, coloured fabric shirt with collar, tie, reddish-brown shoes, no hat.'

2

But the story really begins three weeks before that encounter in Globus. To be precise, in Stuttgart on 18 November 1933. The city is swathed in fog, the elm trees are dark and damp. Grey-faced civil servants are walking across Schillerplatz with their greasy briefcases, unemployed men shivering outside the labour exchange, their wives scouting for winter vegetables in the municipal market. Parked in a vineyard on the city's western outskirts is a small 1930s sports car, a 750 cc BMW Dixi whose owner reported its theft to the police the day before. The bonnet and black leather hood are beaded with dew. Asleep inside the car are two young men, their faces almost invisible betwixt coat collar and hat brim. The youth in the driver's seat is tall and thin. His gangling limbs have spread out inside the car like tentacles. His companion is short and wiry. While sleeping he has drawn up his legs and subsided against the driver's chest. And because the night was so long and so cold, he has snuggled ever closer to him like a girl.

Crows have been attracted by the scraps of food lying scattered on either side of the Dixi – breadcrumbs, six strips of bacon rind and quite a lot of cheese rind, as the police discover that afternoon. The shorter of the two young men in the car wakes up. He moves away from his friend, wipes the condensation off the passenger window with his sleeve, and looks out at the morning, which is aflutter with crows. His eyes are as green as a cat's. To shoo the crows away, he opens the door and closes it again. The birds fly off in a wide arc, making for another vineyard, and the other youth wakes up.

'Morning, Waldemar.'

'Morning, Kurt.'

Kurt Sandweg and Waldemar Velte ceremoniously shake hands the way they do every morning. They began doing this for fun a few years ago, when they were still children playing at being grown-ups, and the habit has simply persisted.

Meantime, on the east side of town, Julius Feuerstein, manager of the Stuttgart Bank's Gablenberg branch, is starting work for the day. First, he pulls on his oversleeves and checks the contents of the cash drawer. Then he tops up the inkwell, examines his pen nibs, and readies the blotting paper and pounce. He puts the sealing wax, inkpad and erasers in their proper places, sharpens the pencils, and changes the date on the rubber stamp. Then he steps back to inspect his handiwork, adjusts his collar, tie and jacket, and twirls his moustache. The roaring, coal-fired stove in the corner is filling the banking hall with fuggy warmth. Feuerstein sits down on the edge of his chair, straight as a ramrod, picks up a file, and opens it.

Hanging above his desk is a gilt-framed portrait photograph of the Führer, who stares down with folded arms and jutting chin at a mousy-looking, round-shouldered little man whose workplace is situated in a gloomy corner of the banking hall. This is a clerk named Gottfried Lindner, Feuerstein's sole subordinate, who has grown old in 32 years' service with the Stuttgarter Bank. Lindner has already become inured to Feuerstein, the peppy young Nazi who has managed the branch for the past six months – rather too peppily for Lindner's taste, and there are occasions when he thinks nostalgically of his long-time boss, who – without explanation – failed to turn up for work from one day to the next. However, Feuerstein did unwittingly introduce a source of secret amusement on his very first day in the job, when he hung the Führer's portrait on the wall. For there is one thing the peppy branch manager doesn't know and cannot tell from where he sits: the stovepipe's route from stove to chimney neatly bisects the Führer's forehead – at least when seen from Lindner's position. And if Lindner cranes his neck just a little, the Führer's piercing eyes are likewise obscured by the rusty stovepipe, leaving visible only his weak chin and sour little schoolmarmish mouth.

'Lindner, coffee!'

Lindner gets to his feet. He has received the order to fetch coffee at 8:35 every day for 32 years. For 32 years he has called back 'Yes, sir!', crossed Wagenburgstrasse to the café opposite, and returned with a tray bearing two cups, saucers and spoons, a sugar bowl, two pots of coffee, and a little jug of cream. Never once in all those 32 years has he failed to perform this errand, except in the summer of 1918 when Kaiser Wilhelm, after much hesitation, decided to dispatch him to the Western Front for the last few months of the war. On 7 August, Lindner was unlucky enough to be hit by a shell splinter. Ever since then he has dragged his left foot a little and has sensed when snow is imminent.

Lindner and Feuerstein stir their coffees without exchanging a word. Lindner does this silently and with due decorum, secretly but intensely irritated every morning by the unabashed tinkle of Feuerstein's spoon against his cup. The wall clock ticks away loudly and dependably. Then comes the sound of an approaching car. It dies away immediately outside the entrance.

Feuerstein stations himself at the counter and looks at the door in expectation of the day's first client, while Lindner disappears into the back room with the tray. It's quite likely to be pretty Frau Niemayer, who drives up every Saturday to draw out her pin money from an account her lord and master knows nothing about. They're like that, these so-called ladies from the prosperous suburbs, who climb out of who knows whose soft bed with their cheeks chafed raw by another man's stubbly chin and then roll up here as if it were the most natural thing in the world! Last Saturday, for example, the Niemayer woman had stood in front of Feuerstein's counter in her feather boa and brazenly tweaked her brassière straight while he was making out the withdrawal receipt. She watched his pen travel over the paper with an air of indifference, and then, when he deliberately barked 'There, that's done!' (to bring the woman to her senses, humiliate her, and make it clear to her how shamelessly she was behaving in the presence of a man), she had looked him wearily in the eye and scratched her hip with her long red fingernails.

Feuerstein clears his throat and hides his half-empty cup in the top drawer of his desk, where he keeps a corner free for that particular purpose. When the swing door opens, it isn't pretty Frau Niemayer who enters the bank but two pale-faced young men – well-dressed young men in knickerbockers and expensive tweed overcoats, with their hair slicked back.

'Good morning gentlemen. How can I be of service?'

There's a pistol already pointing at Feuerstein's head. Staring fixedly at him over the barrel is the shorter of the two young men, who has green eyes. He doesn't speak. His companion, a lanky fellow, has no gun; he simply stands there with an air of embarrassment. Feuerstein waits to see what happens next. Since neither of the newcomers says anything, he opens the cash drawer and deposits a wad of banknotes on the counter: 25 fifties, or 1250 Reichsmarks. The drawer contains several more wads of hundreds, twenties and tens.

The tall young man picks up the wad, stuffs it in his coat pocket, says 'Many thanks!', sketches a bow, and tips his hat in farewell. Feuerstein is puzzled. Is he making fun of him? No. He actually seems content with what he's been given, although there's so much more money there for the taking. Very odd. But the short, green-eyed young man continues to point his gun straight at Feuerstein. He isn't joking. He wants more.

In the back room, old Lindner has registered none of this. He deliberately finishes his coffee, sets the cup down silently on the tray, straightens his jacket and tie, and limps out into the banking hall. Everyone gives a start: Lindner at the gun pointing at Feuerstein's head; the two bank robbers at Lindner's unexpected appearance; and Feuerstein at the startled expression on the robbers' faces. The shock travels from person to person like a squirrel scampering up a tree, and when it gets back to Lindner he gives another start, whereupon they all follow suit and a 7.65 mm bullet leaves the gun. It pierces Feuerstein's forehead and the back of his skull explodes. Julius Feuerstein, 27 years old and unmarried, member of the National Socialist Brownshirts, of the Householders' and Landowners' Association, of the Gablenberg Athletics Club, of the Snowshoe Section of the Swabian Alps Association and the Auto-Union, is already dead when he pulls out the open cash drawer in falling. Mark and pfennig coins shower down on him; the banknotes remain in the drawer because they're held in place by spring clips.

Lindner hares into the back room. A second shot rings out, then a third, fourth, fifth and sixth. Wood splinters and plaster spurts, but Lindner makes it to the red button unscathed and presses it for the first time in 32 years' service. Outside, the alarm bell starts to shrill.

❧

Many years later, the spot where Julius Feuerstein died will be occupied by two white desks with two white computers on them. A bank no longer, the building houses a travel agency. Hanging on the walls are photographic blow-ups of Bali, Mexico and Spitzbergen, and colourful brochures with last-minute offers are displayed in the window. Seated at the desks are two friendly young women. When you tell them about the bank raid, they simultaneously look down at the floor as if drops of blood may still be detectable on the needle-felt carpet. 'You don't say!' they exclaim in unison.

❧

Eyewitnesses unanimously testified that the door burst open and the bank robbers came dashing out; that the shorter of the two came to a halt and aimed his pistol at the nearest pedestrians; that his companion got into the Dixi, inserted the key in the ignition and tried to start the car; that the engine refused to start because the starter motor turned the engine over far too slowly, draining the battery, until the robber with the pistol shouted: 'Stop that, I'll push you!' He then braced his left shoulder against the doorframe, keeping the gun levelled at the passers-by with his right hand. Talstrasse is on a slope, so the Dixi quickly picked up speed. The young man with the gun climbed on to the running board, the car gave a lurch, and the engine caught.

❧

My grandfather was a taciturn man. He never spoke on principle when Grandmother was within earshot, and when he did become talkative – for instance when pruning the sour cherry trees far from the house in early February – he carefully avoided Grandmother's women's talk. He was a schoolmaster. His area was facts and his knowledge encyclopaedic: orchard and garden pest control, the social behaviour of foxes and crows, the orbital periods of the moons of Jupiter, the history of the automobile. 'I never drove a Dixi myself, but they were very popular in those days. A small car of British design. Nippy but not overly expensive. BMW built it under licence from 1928 onwards – at the Eisenach Works, if I remember correctly. Straight-4 cylinders, 748.5cc engine capacity, vertical valves, just short of 15 horsepower, maximum speed 100 kilometres per hour. One weak point was the A-shaped ladder-frame chassis with fixed axles suspended in front on cross-leaf springs and behind on quarter elliptical springs, which made the Dixi tend to drift on bends. All the same, it was quite successful as a racing car. It won the Coupe des Alpes in 1929 and the 750 class of the Monte Carlo Rally.'

❧

After 500 metres the Dixi turned off left down Abelsbergstrasse and first right into Luisenstrasse, a quiet little cul-de-sac flanked by gardens and small, two-storeyed working-class homes. Upstairs in Number 38 a woman was hanging some bedclothes out of the window to air. Puzzled to see an unfamiliar car pull up in her street, she debated whether to note down the licence number: III A 17668. Still in two minds, she stepped back from the window and drew the curtains, but too late: the driver of the car had spotted her. He looked up and smiled. He had a very friendly smile, you had to give him that. The woman peered round the curtains and watched to see what would happen next. The friendly young man started talking and gesticulating; she noticed only now that someone else was sitting in the passenger seat, only his legs and stomach being visible. The two of them seemed to be arguing. The woman regretted her ability to hear what was said. The nice young man looked as if he was angry with his companion, who appeared to be defending himself. After a while the gesticulations ceased and silence fell inside the car. Then the nice young man took off his hat and, still inside the cramped little car, not only peeled off his overcoat and jacket but removed his shoes and knickerbockers as well. The man in the passenger seat did likewise. Then the pair changed into some different clothes that had evidently been lying ready to hand on the back seat. Strange. The woman decided that she must definitely write down the licence number.

The young men seemed in no hurry at all, she would tell Detective Superintendent Wilhelm Schneider, who was heading the investigation, when interviewed the next morning. In a leisurely, unhurried manner and with absolutely no sign of urgency, they had ambled down the steps at the end of the cul-de-sac and into Kanonenweg with their original clothes draped neatly over their arms. While descending the steps, the shorter of the two had given the tall young man, the nice one, a soothing pat on the back. The latter had then done the same to his shorter companion.

Detective Superintendent Schneider says goodbye to the woman, then makes his way down the steps and into Kanonenweg, which leads in the direction of the city centre. At the next intersection he looks left. In the distance he can make out the bank building, now without any police cars parked outside. It is quite possible that the robbers paused at this very spot and watched the police taking up the pursuit with all the manpower at their disposal, heading out of town. They would have stood there with their clothes draped neatly over their arms. They must be cheeky young devils. Cheeky and cold-blooded.

Detective Superintendent Schneider sets off again. If they've escaped into town they must have gone to ground somewhere. He walks past the New Palace and the Old Castle, heading for the old quarter of the city. Passing the town hall, he makes for the youth hostel in Torstrasse. Schneider finds the warden polishing pans in the kitchen. He conceals a baffled smile behind his moustache. These Swabians! Fancy standing in the kitchen early on a Sunday morning, polishing pans as if it were the most enjoyable thing in the world! The warden is not only freshly shaven but as rosy-cheeked and cheerful as he has been every morning of his 50 years on earth. Schneider will never understand this South German *joie de vivre*. He hails from Hamburg and only got himself transferred here for his wife's sake when they were both young and slim and newly in love.

The warden deposits two cups of coffee on the kitchen table. Schneider opens the visitors' book. The most recent entry reads: 'Kurt Sandweg and Waldemar Velte, both born 1910, arr. from Wuppertal, left for Ulm and Munich 19 November.'

'These two. Have they really gone already?'

'First thing this morning, I'm afraid. I heard the stairs creak, but that was all. Thoroughly nice lads.'

Superintendent Schneider gets to his feet and buttons his overcoat, intending to return to headquarters at once and initiate a manhunt.

But the warden catches his arm.

'They can't possibly be your bank robbers.'

'Why not?'

'For one thing, because they've very little money. They even asked me for a discount. I gave them one, of course. Very nice lads.'

'And?'

'For another, they both made a reliable, respectable impression. Kurt Sandweg especially. There was something trustworthy about his face, know what I mean? Then there was their decent clothes and their Rhineland dialect ...'

The warden defends his guests with such conviction that Superintendent Schneider notes down a whole bunch of names from the visitors' book, but not those of Sandweg and Velte. This is the warden's bad luck, because a reward of 1000 Reichsmarks has just been posted this Sunday morning for information leading to the arrest of the Gablenberg bank robbers.

3

For hour after hour an open lorry jolts along northwards through the narrow interstice between the overcast sky and the autumnally brown countryside. Seated in the back, which is empty, are Kurt Sandweg and Waldemar Velte. They have pulled their hats down over their faces and turned up their coat collars. For protection from the icy headwind, they are sitting huddled close together, shoulder to shoulder, against the back of the driver's cab. Velte has tossed his pistol into the bushes somewhere. The road follows the course of the mighty Rhine for many kilometres. Barges with never-drying laundry pegged to lines on deck greet one another in passing with blasts on their foghorns. Proud palaces and castles look down from the heights at the respectable middle-class homes beside the river.

At last the road diverges from the Rhine. The light begins to fade here at four in the afternoon. In the west, the jagged black spires of Cologne Cathedral glide slowly past, and then Waldemar and Kurt are back home in Wuppertal, which despite its 400,000 inhabitants is not a proper city so much as a series of gloomy, Depression-blighted industrial towns clustered together in a narrow valley. It is possible that, many centuries ago, the Wupper was a clear little river flowing through a charming valley, but then it turned out that its lime- and iron-free water was ideally suited to the textile industry. Today it's a foaming brown broth flanked by serried rows of factories, half of which have closed down since the stock market crash of 1929. High above the river hums the famous suspended monorail, a miraculous welded structure begun in the previous century. The north wind is blowing clouds of coal-black smoke along the streets, and it's November.

The lorry skirts the Wupper for kilometres. It is nearing the eastern outskirts of the city when the driver glances enquiringly at his passengers through the rear window. At last Waldemar raps on the cab's metal roof and the vehicle pulls up. He and Kurt wave goodbye and jump down off the back of the lorry. They are in the middle of Berliner Platz, not far from the north-east edge of town, where industrialists' Art Nouveau mansions look out on pastureland and beech woods. They walk on uphill together for a while, then shake hands in farewell.

Waldemar opens the garden gate and slinks round the house. He's in luck: the back door isn't locked. The flickering light of an open fire is reflected by the walls of the passage. Beside the fireplace in the living room, Waldemar's ten-year-old brother Lothar is standing in front of his mother, who is adjusting the fit of his brand-new uniform. His father isn't there; a building contractor, he's working day and night to save his firm from bankruptcy. Seated cross-legged on the sofa in the background is Hilde, Waldemar's thirteen-year-old sister. 'That was the last time we three children were together,' she will say nearly seven decades later. 'One doesn't forget things like that. I also recall what I was reading that evening: *Pünktchen und Anton* by Erich Kästner. It hadn't been out long.'

Little Lothar has pulled his cap down over his forehead. On his belt is a sheath knife adorned with the smart black, white and red swastika emblem. The blade is engraved with the words 'Blood and Honour'. When Waldemar comes in, Lothar shoots out his arm and points to him. His childish face becomes convulsed with rage.

'Waldemar! Don't say anything! Not a word, you hear?'

'Good evening,' says Waldemar. His mother smiles uneasily. Hilde continues to sit quietly on the sofa and puts the book on her lap.

'Waldemar!' Lothar shouts with his arm still outstretched. Then, pursing his lips and lowering his arm, he stomps past Waldemar, slams the door, and goes to his room. Waldemar kisses his mother and flops down in a leather armchair.

'So you bought him the uniform after all.'

'The winter outfit, yes.'

'Very smart.'

'What else could I do? I didn't buy him the summer outfit or the sports kit although the boy went on at me for months. Last Thursday, though, his squad leader came to the door. He glared at me sternly and demanded to know why Lothar was still turning up for parade in civvies.'

'What did you say?'

'I told him our construction business was doing badly and we had no money. And do you know what the youngster did then? He looked me up and down in an insolent way and said: "Really? There was just enough for you, though, huh?"'

Waldemar gets up and puts a log on the fire.

'Leave the boy alone, will you?' she said. 'They're all in it these days, you know – all of them, honestly. You should see them on Saturdays, when they go marching out of town and into the woods.'

'Yes, I know. The tramp of marching feet, the shining eyes, the drums and fanfares. The songs and banners.'

'At least they never get bored, what with all that marching and camping and those excursions and evening classes. And Lothar has become much stronger physically.'

Waldemar gets to his feet. 'Please excuse me, Mother. Kurt and I are leaving tomorrow morning.'

'Again? Where for?'

'Königswinter with the Rhine steamer and then on to the Felsensee. Some friends of ours are camping there. They're expecting us.'

'Camping? In November?'

'We don't mind.'

'Waldemar?'

'Yes?'

'Have you been looking for a job?'

'Industry is suffering from 40 per cent unemployment, Mother, and the few jobs available are earmarked for Party members.'

'Then go to the labour exchange.'

Waldemar's sister Hilde has been listening to their conversation in silence. She will remember her brother's parting words for the rest of her life. 'No, no, a hundred times no. The Labour Corps camp in the Marscheider Forest, maybe, or lumberjacking for Public Welfare? I won't lift a finger to assist those criminals.'

At dawn the next day Waldemar steals downstairs carrying his small leather suitcase. His mother is lying awake and listening to his footsteps. His brother is lying awake and listening to his footsteps. His sister is also awake and listening. Waldemar leaves by way of the front door, which is framed by some massive, rough-hewn blocks of stone. The blocks above the door are pierced by a circular, leaded window about a metre in diameter with a stained-glass coat of arms in it. The house is Father Velte's rocky fortress, the impregnable stronghold he built his family as a refuge from the world – except that now the world has only to send a pubescent squad leader or an onion-breathed liquidator, and his wife and children are as defenceless as hares in open countryside.

Waldemar makes his way up the steep street to the cross-roads where Kurt is waiting, also with a small leather suitcase. Some months ago, Waldemar was roughed up at this cross-roads for having said 'Good morning' instead of uttering the government-prescribed form of salutation. As he lay curled up on the ground, a 'People's Comrade' stuck a gun muzzle in his mouth while two others, whom he knew from grammar school, knelt beside him and shouted 'Enemy of the State! Enemy of the State!' in his ears. He could still taste the gun oil days later.

Waldemar Velte and Kurt Sandweg walk down to the mon-orail station together. That they've absolutely no intention of camping beside the Felsensee goes without saying.

ꝭ

Hilde Velte thought again and again about her brother's long journey. 'I believe they meant to go to America or India. We had an uncle who worked as an engineer on a tea plantation. Kurt and Waldemar wanted to go there. They couldn't stand it at home any longer. My brother was a serious person, cheerful but melancholy at the same time. He read a lot of Nietzsche and Schopenhauer, which can hardly have raised his spirits. Once he even tried to sport a great big moustache, but it didn't grow much. When the business with the Nazis started, he was in absolute despair. Kurt, on the other hand, had a sunny nature. He probably went with Waldemar just because he was his best friend. Kurt was a Sunday's child. He'd have been happy anywhere, no matter where.'

But travelling to India is a complicated matter. Since the Great War, civil servants have seized power with their rubber stamps and forms and regulations. 'You want a visa for Belgium? That you can get in Cologne. A transit visa for France? Why do you need one if you're going to Belgium? Just in case? Oh well, it's up to you. If you don't mind the palaver – but the French consulate is in Düsseldorf! Have you got Certificates X and Y with you? I'm sorry, those you must get from the municipal authorities in your place of residence, in, er, Wuppertal – yes, that's right, stamped by the Residents' Registration Bureau and the police. In triplicate, yes, like I told you. Oh, you again! What's this, though? The date's missing. Sorry, you'll have to go back to, er, Wuppertal. That's right … No, I can't fill in the date myself, what are you thinking of? That would be documentary falsification and abuse of office. Next time, bring three passport photos with you, plus twelve Reichsmarks and a copy of your citizenship certificate, got it? Then we'll fill in the application form right away and forward it to … '

It goes on like this for four days. Kurt and Waldemar dash from city to city, roam through unfamiliar, flag-bedecked parts of town in search of this or that government office, and wait submissively on hard wooden benches in long, freshly waxed corridors, only to find that office hours ended just before their turn came and the janitor shoos them out into the street with his broom. They spend the night in creaking beds in bleak, bug-ridden boarding houses. If police sirens rend the night somewhere, they wake up with a start. In the end, though, everything goes smoothly and they cross the German-Belgian frontier at Aachen.

4

Antwerp, 24 November 1933. The harbour smells alluringly of diesel fumes, rotting fish, lubricating oil and fresh sea air. The rotary luffing cranes reach out into the fog like prehistoric insects. Vessels of all sizes are lying at anchor. The piers and quays are teeming with people: seamen on shore leave, dockers, longshoremen, warehousemen, crane drivers, weighers and measurers, tugmen, hawsermen, ship's cleaners, and, of course, wealthy passengers with their fur coats, top hats and porters. A liner looms up alongside the quay like a steel mountain. The ship's engines throb, the water in the harbour basin froths, two wharfers let go the hawsers. The gap between the quay and the ship's side widens. High above, pale faces stare into space and many passengers wave goodbye to the Old Continent. The ship's orchestra beneath the Chinese lanterns on the promenade deck plays a waltz. Screeching seagulls carry the music out to sea.

The ship is sailing without Kurt and Waldemar. First, because they don't have the requisite papers, secondly because America already has 15 million unemployed without them, and thirdly because the 1250 Reichsmarks from the bank raid are nowhere near enough. They are now sitting on a coil of rope on the quayside, reading a newspaper.

PAGE ONE: Thousands of unemployed steelworkers and

coal miners are streaming towards the capital from the whole of Northern France. They are marching in groups of no more than five men because the police have prohibited any mass demonstrations. The roads to Paris from Calais, Lille and Roubaix are under strict surveillance.

MISCELLANEOUS REPORTS: In the Scottish Highlands, photographer Hugh Gray is the first to take pictures of a lizard-like creature in a mist-enshrouded lake called Loch Ness.

GERMANY: Reich Commissioner Hermann Göring is speeding up the construction of government concentration camps. He wants to gain control over the activities of the Brownshirts, who are running unauthorised camps on their own initiative. Vehement protests are being voiced throughout the country, in nationalist quarters as well, about their brutal resort to torture and murder.

INTERNATIONAL: More and more European and North American banks are being raided every year. Bank robbers are profiting from the technological advantage fast cars give them over the ill-equipped police. Moreover, the removal of even large sums of cash has presented no great problem ever since paper money became the principal form of currency during the inflation of 1922/3.

SPORT: The German national football team has beaten the Swiss side two–nil in front of 30,000 spectators in Zurich's Hardturm Stadium. The goals were scored in the last 20 minutes by Lachner and Hohmann.

ACCIDENTS AND CRIMES: In the south-western United States, a gangster couple are carrying out sanguinary raids on banks, jewellers', gas stations – even butchers' shops. On 8 November Clyde Barrow and Bonnie Parker raid the payroll office of the McMurray Oil Refinery in Arp, Texas. On 21 November, after a shoot-out with the sheriff and his deputies at Grand Prairie, they escape in a stolen Ford V8. Bonnie is 23 years old, Clyde 24.

And here is a report from Stuttgart: 'The great and sincere sympathy felt by wide sections of the population at the terrible stroke of fate that has befallen the family of the murder victim was once more movingly demonstrated at the hour of farewell beside Julius Feuerstein's grave. Several thousand mourners gathered around his last resting place. The coffin was displayed in the mortuary with members of the Gablenberg Athletics Club standing vigil. Comrades from the Athletics Club then bore the coffin containing their beloved member's mortal remains to the grave along the cemetery's main thoroughfare, which was flanked by an honour guard of athletes. Preceding the coffin were the crêpe-adorned flags of the Labour Front, and the Gablenberg athletes were followed by the deceased's comrades in the SA with their black-swathed flag, who were in turn followed by many mourners bearing wreaths.'

The ocean liner leaves the harbour basin and Kurt Sandweg and Waldemar Velte go straight back to the station. They catch the night train to Paris via Brussels the same evening.

5

There are only new arrivals at the Gare de l'Est; no one is departing. Day after day, dozens of west-bound trains pull in and hundreds of people make for the exit through clouds of steam from the locomotives. Many have brought heavy cabin trunks and employ porters to carry them, many trundle whole mountains of bags and suitcases along the platform on worn-out perambulators, and many possess no luggage at all. Sandweg and Velte carry their own leather suitcases. An unending tide of humanity pours into the big city. All the hotels and guesthouses have long been booked up, and absurd prices are being charged for the draughtiest attic rooms. After a few hours, anyone short of luck and money inevitably ends up in the slums on the city's outskirts. Many are eager to work and bring up their children there, many form committees and found journals, many simply survive, and many will sometime lie down on the bed in their room and swallow a bottle of pills, and their last sight of this world will be the grimy wall-paper on the opposite wall or the rain-swept tin roof across the courtyard.

'What were my brother and Kurt looking for there? Nothing

at all. Paris isn't on the sea, it was just a stepping stone on the way to Marseille. Waldemar sent us a picture postcard with the Eiffel Tower on the front. He was rather sarcastic about Paris. Surrealist exhibitions, boxing matches, men wearing make-up, scrawny girls in short, beaded skirts – it wasn't his scene. I mean, neither of them could speak French. There definitely wasn't anyone eager to welcome two unemployed lads from Wuppertal. They also had to be careful with their money because it was meant to last them all the way to India.'

Kurt and Waldemar did what all provincial youngsters do on their first visit to Paris: they roamed the city for hours, from Sacré-Cœur to the Eiffel Tower and on to the Luxembourg Gardens and the Latin Quarter, Notre Dame, the Bastille, Père Lachaise, and so on; they stared admiringly after the middle-class *Parisiennes* who had the knack of swaying their hips in such a sophisticated, elegant, blasé manner; they eyed the windows of luxury shops that had ceased to display any prices; they ate steak and *frites* twice a day and invariably got told off by a waiter whose complexion portended a gastric ulcer; they inspected the prostitutes in the Place Pigalle at night; and, after a few days, they grew sick of the city's self-importance and were glad they didn't have to live there.

The icy wind from Siberia was making its annual winter journey across the Polar Sea at this time. It normally blows westwards to Greenland, far to the north, but at Advent 1933

it turned south in Russia. A wave of air as cold as minus 32 degrees Centigrade swept over Bulgaria, Hungary and Yugoslavia to France. Dozens of homeless people froze to death in Sofia, Budapest and Belgrade. In Paris it began to snow heavily.

On their seventh day there, Waldemar and Kurt board the Basel express at the Gare de l'Est and sit down side by side in a third-class compartment, inseparable as ever. Stowed in the luggage net above their heads are their suitcases and – their only souvenir of Paris – a portable wind-up gramophone. The journey will take eight hours. They will see little of the countryside because the train hasn't gone far before the windows are coated with fern frost millimetres thick.

'Homosexual? You've got the wrong idea about them, especially Kurt. If ever a man liked girls, it was him. What's more, they liked him too. I myself was a little bit in love with him, although he was far too old for me. A lot of girls were scared of Waldemar because he was so serious. But it's true the two of them had an intimate relationship. During those last few months, Kurt and Waldemar were together all the time. They lived together, actually: sometimes a few days at our place, then a few days at the Sandwegs', then back with us. Our parents weren't too happy about it, because it really was a bit odd, but what could they do? Besides, we were all fond of Kurt. He was like one of the family.'

6

My maternal grandparents were born and raised and spent their whole lives in a village in Basel's hinterland, nestling among the last gentle foothills of the Jura, far from the noise and bustle of the city. The area is famed for its cherry brandy, and the hills afford a fine view of Alsace in the west and the Black Forest in the north. Whenever Germany and France were at war with each other, the sound of artillery fire came rolling across the mountains like thunder, and at night one could see the lightning flashes of the guns. However, no foreign soldiers had set foot in Basel's hinterland since the Napoleonic Wars.

My grandfather's name was Ernst Walder, and he was the eldest scion of a prosperous farming family whose men had filled the post of village schoolmaster since 1848. He had taken over the job from his father in the mid-1920s because the latter had had enough of the village children's everlasting ignorance. Over the years, Ernst had also succeeded his father as chairman of the men's athletics club and conductor of the Catholic choral association, and he had taken over the seat on the parish council to which the family had been entitled for centuries. At the time of this story, he was also a midfield player in the football club, head of the local civil defence organisation, and a popular deliverer of funeral orations – in addition to being tall, strong, good-looking, 33 years old and unmarried.

Seven years younger, my grandmother was a buxom and curvaceous blonde and the only daughter of an equally prosperous farming family that had also run the post office and the *Zur Traube* restaurant since time immemorial. Marie Stifter could play the piano and had learnt French in Lausanne, and she would sooner or later inherit a substantial quantity of building land.

Ernst Walder and Marie Stifter were by far the most eligible couple of their generation in the village: upstanding scions of two long-established families that were not too closely related and had hitherto provoked no scandals of any kind. It was clear to the entire village that the pair were destined for each other, and they themselves seem to have realised this, albeit in a curiously joyless, dutiful way. True, he came to collect her Sunday after Sunday and they would walk across the fields arm in arm; true, he danced as exclusively with her at village functions as she did with him; true, he regularly paid courtesy calls at the post office and the *Traube*; true, she stood behind the opposing team's goal whenever the football club was playing; and true, she adorned the assembly room with the other members' wives whenever the athletics club held a soirée; but they did all these things in a far too methodical way and without any real enthusiasm. When out walking they never strode harmoniously along in step like a happy couple, but kept bumping into each other with their elbows and hip bones; on the dance floor they comported themselves in such a wooden, clumsy manner that one couldn't help feeling sorry for them; and when they looked into each other's eyes, it was always with distaste and mistrust. But they were a couple despite this, and both families waited with quiet confidence for Ernst to pop the long-overdue question. If he hadn't done so before, it was doubtless because he had so much on his plate. The pair were simply made for each other, and that was that.

Their relationship became no more passionate when, at Christmas 1933, Marie took a job as a temporary shop assistant. Ernst was surprised that this well-off, pampered young woman should, in return for a meagre wage, take on such a chore: getting up well before dawn and walking to the next village, travelling by bus to the neighbouring town and from there, wedged in with thousands of other country folk, by train to Basel; dancing attendance on hoity-toity city folk all day long; and returning by the same route each evening.

Ernst Walder was no fool. He realised that the job at Globus was probably the one chance in her life Marie would ever have of escaping the narrow confines of the village, the family and matrimony, so he raised no objection. For one thing, they weren't officially engaged, so he had no formal claim on her; secondly, her absence didn't trouble him too greatly; thirdly, he had no objection to her saving some money before their wedding; and, fourthly, he didn't feel jealous, perhaps from lack of imagination.

It so happened, however, that chance (and Globus's personnel manager) assigned Marie to the sports department, of which Ernst was a regular customer. It is on record that on 14 December 1933 he purchased a new Nabholz tracksuit, a black one with two horizontal white stripes across the chest. After he had paid, Marie wrapped up the tracksuit in brown paper while Ernst stood watching her with his hands buried in his trouser pockets.

'By the way,' she said, 'there's a 30 per cent discount today on handball gloves.'

'Thanks, but they're for handball. You can't use them for football.'

'I know. I just thought I'd mention it.'
'Fine.'
'Do you collect our discount stamps?'
'No.'
'You should. It's worth it.'
'If you say so.'
'It certainly is. Do you have a game on Sunday?'
'No, it's the winter break. We start again in February.'
'I see.'
'Yes.'
'By the way, what's-his-name was in here today, the fire chief's son.'
'Really?'
'He bought a bicycle, an expensive one. He's got a doctorate now.'
'A doctorate, pfft!' The day Ernst Walder finally decided in favour of a safe teaching job and against a university education, he had developed a profound aversion to academics. 'What sort of doctorate?'
'Just a doctorate.'
'There are different kinds of doctorates, Marie. Doctors of science focus on science, doctors of jurisprudence focus on the law, and doctors of philology are full of hot air.'
'Yes, yes,' sighed Marie. 'So you've often told me.'
'Well, so long.'
'So long.'
'Shall we travel home together?'
'If you like.'
'When shall I pick you up?'
'At seven. In Marktplatz. At the tram station.'

❧

At the same moment, in the gramophone record department:

'Fräulein Dorly, there you are!'

'Good morning, Fräulein Dorly.'

'Good morning, gentlemen.'

Exactly 24 hours have gone by since their first meeting in Globus's record department. Dorly gives the 'Finn' and the awkward 'Austrian' only a glance. So they really have stayed on an extra day in Basel. Dorly won't have as much time for them today. The two of them overdid it a bit yesterday, with their dancing and their talk of birthdays and first names and star signs. Today she's very busy putting away a new consignment. It has to be done and the sooner the better – Advent is a busy time – but she naturally looks out the record they ordered. Ah, here it is. Of course, if the gentlemen absolutely insist, I can play the record for the first time here in the shop, but I won't be liable for any damage. Dorly deposits the needle in the groove. Hisses and crackles, then the strings strike up *fortissimo* with piano accompaniment. After three bars the orchestra plays more softly and the vocal begins.

I used to like my life the way it was,
and always found it wonderful because
I madly, gladly yielded to its spell.
But, now I've looked deep into a heart like yours,
I've come to realise something all too well:

Into your hands my happiness I give,
it's yours to keep, whatever may befall.
Come joy or grief, however long I live,

yours are my past, my future, and my all.

If fate should smile on me,
I'll bless the day.
But if it turns its back,
I'll simply say:

Be comforting and hold me close,
in your sweet hands I'll find repose.

If fate should smile on me,
I'll bless the day.
But if it turns its back,
I'll simply say:

Be comforting and hold me close,
in your sweet hands I'll find repose.

Dorly watches the little Finn, who listens to the soft, melancholy tango with his arms at his sides and his eyes half-closed. So that was his kind of music. Dorly wouldn't have thought it. 'I had more faith in the two of them after we'd played *In Deine Hände,* Velte especially. He didn't strike me as so grim; on the contrary, he seemed sensitive and defenceless – rather mixed-up as well, perhaps.'

Dorly no longer wants the two young men to leave as soon as possible. She puts on another Willi Kollo record, then another and another and another: *Warum hast Du so traurige Augen?, Jetzt geht's der Dolly gut, Mach mit mir eine Mondscheinfahrt, Ich kenn' zwei süsse Schwestern, Lieber Leierkastenmann.*

Lunchtime is over far too quickly. The record department

fills up with customers, and Dorly has no more time to spare. The young men have to go. 'Before leaving, Velte ordered another record we didn't have in stock; I think it was *Grüss mir mein Hawaii,* also sung by Willi Kollo. We again agreed that he could collect it the next day.'

Young men do sometimes linger in the record department for a noticeably long time. Dorly knows what they like about her: her straight back, her slim hips, and the fact that she doesn't spend the whole day simpering behind the counter. A few years ago she accepted two or three invitations to go for a walk or have a coffee. No longer, though. It was the same thing every time and meant nothing, and even if it had for once meant something, she didn't want it. Two years with Anton were more than enough for her. But this little German is different. He says what he wants, no more and no less.

'Please, Fräulein Dorly, I'd like to go on with our conversation. Would you meet us this evening?'

'Both of you?' Dorly asks, amused. The two of them seem inseparable.

'Yes.'

'All right, why not? After closing time, seven o'clock. In Marktplatz, by the advertising pillar.'

'We'll be there.'

'I may bring a girlfriend with me, if that's all right. I don't know if she'll come, though. I'll ask.'

The girlfriend is an assistant in the sports department. 'Friend' is something of an exaggeration, perhaps, but she likes the ebullient country girl far better than all the other shop assistants. She isn't as boring as those silly Basel cows, whose heads are full of nothing but silk stockings, declarations of love and wedding dresses.

The shop shuts two hours after darkness falls. Dorly Schupp and Marie Stifter emerge into the Christmas glitter of Marktplatz. Men and women are heading for home laden with gift parcels of all sizes. The Rheinbrücke Department Store's Santa Claus has flown away in his biplane, the children have long since gone home. Fräulein Friendly is warming her numb limbs in the nearest café. Seated across the table from her is the head of advertising. Or the head of department.

❧

Ernst Walder is waiting at the tram station. He sees Marie, arm-in-arm with a strange young woman, go over to two unknown men standing beside the advertising pillar. Well-dressed young men in knickerbockers. Regular dandies. Ernst is astonished. Hasn't Marie seen him, has she forgotten their arrangement? Should he wave to her, go after her? No. He can tell from the set of her neck that she has neither forgotten about nor failed to see him, and that it's all she can do not to look at him. He waits to see what happens next.

❧

'Hello, Fräulein Dorly. How nice of you to come – with a friend, too.' Dorly shakes hands with them both, then introduces Marie Stifter. Once more, the tall young man does all the talking; his shorter companion stands beside him looking sombre. Marie, who finds the latter unnerving, is surprised that Dorly Schupp has a thing for him. She rather regrets having come, although the tall, slim boy seems quite nice. Anyway, they'll both be long gone by tomorrow, Dorly said. To Spain or even further away, so nothing much can happen.

'May we invite you for a coffee?'

'Would you care for something to eat?'

'Would you like to go to the pictures?'

'The theatre?'

'Dancing?'

'The fairground?'

'A concert, perhaps?'

'Shall we listen to some records in our hotel room?'

Marie Stifter is delighted. She'd like to accept all these invitations at once and in any kind of order, but Dorly rejects the lot.

'From the start, I didn't want to do anything with those two Germans that might have led to a so-called affair,' Dorly will say when questioned. 'I had no designs on them and wanted things to remain that way from their point of view as well. Besides, I knew they'd be leaving the next day or the day after that.'

So the foursome go for a harmless walk. Kurt and Marie take the lead with Dorly and Waldemar following a few paces behind.

Ernst Walder continues to stand at the tram station, gazing after them until they disappear down Eisengasse. He knows there's nothing he can decently do at this stage. After all, he isn't officially engaged to Marie, still less married to her. That is nobody's fault but his own, so he has no right to go running after her.

The Siberian wind has been raging in Basel for days now. Fountains and streams have frozen over and millions of needle-sharp ice crystals are blowing across the Rhine. Dorly, Marie, Kurt and Waldemar are relatively sheltered while still in Eisengasse, but on the Central Bridge the north wind hits them in the face and tugs at their hats and coats. It buffets their skirts and trousers and tousles their hair, and ice crystals infiltrate their ears, noses and mouths.

'Kurt Sandweg was a cheerful soul – I nicknamed him Bajazzo the Clown. That first evening, for instance, he walked three or four paces ahead of us in the middle of the bridge, turned around, and opened his overcoat wide. Then he invited Waldemar Velte, Marie Stifter and myself to come under his wing. Since he was nearly two metres tall, his coat protected us really well from the wind. Then all four of us walked backwards across the bridge facing away from the wind. Marie and I on Sandweg's left and Waldemar Velte on his right.'

The wind is blowing less fiercely in Kleinbasel, on the north bank of the Rhine, than on the bridge. It turns into a long walk. They don't take the riverside path but walk along the 20-metre-wide banks of gravel that have formed this winter because the level of the Rhine is unusually low. It's as if the water has emigrated. Lying on the riverbed are encrusted lavatory bowls, rusty murder weapons and old bicycles overgrown with waterweed, and the frozen gravel is slippery and smells of the sea. On both sides of the river the banks are reinforced with walls composed of huge limestone blocks that glow white in the darkness.

Dorly and Waldemar walk side by side like two carriage horses. They glance at each other from time to time. 'Velte claimed they were in transit. His father was a building contractor, and they had to go to Spain because of some forthcoming building jobs. They had broken their journey in Basel, he said, because they had to wait there for a report that was due any day. That information was enough for me, so I didn't question him further. I'd forgotten about all their talk of having to move on at once the first time we met in Globus.'

Kurt takes Marie by the hand and walks on ahead with her. He leads her along a landing stage to a moored rowing boat and rocks it until water washes over the gunwale; he pushes her off balance and catches her before she falls in, then holds her in his arms a moment too long; he imitates the mating call of a duck, waves to Dorly and Waldemar and returns to the river bank, skims flat pebbles across the water and tries to teach Marie to do the same; climbs up on to the Dreirosen Bridge, which is under construction, its steel girders abruptly stopping short in the middle of the river, with Marie flitting after him wherever he goes. Then the two of them climb on to the derrick mounted on the stub end of the bridge and she only just manages to persuade him not to climb out on to the jib.

Marie doesn't know what's happening to her. She has never been for a walk like this before. This German is leading her blithely through the darkness, and he always seems to know in advance whether she wants to turn right or left or stand still; when she thinks of taking out her handkerchief, he hands her one – a clean one, what's more – and when she stumbles on the slippery gravel he's there in a flash to support her. And he can talk. Occasionally they perch on a frozen bench to catch their breath, then Waldemar and Dorly catch them up and join them. It's cold and late. The wind is bitter and their feet are aching. The lights in the windows of the houses round about are going out one by one.

'Not too bored, Fräulein Dorly?' asks Kurt.

'We're getting on fine, don't worry.'

'Is he talking to you, at least? Hey, are you talking to Fräulein Dorly, or just staring into the dark water all the time?' Kurt puts his arm round Waldemar's shoulders and gives him a vigorous hug. 'Do as I do, Fräulein Dorly: use brute force, it's the only way. Pump him about something – the Wuppertal monorail, say. He knows all about that. Shall we walk on, Fraülein Marie? Shall I escort you to the station?'

Kurt Sandweg takes Marie by the hand and disappears into the darkness with her. Dorly and Waldemar stay behind on the bench. There's a long silence.

Then Dorly whispers, '*Is* there a monorail in Wuppertal?'

Waldemar shuffles his feet on the gravel. 'It's world-famous, at least in Wuppertal. A horizontal Eiffel Tower, so to speak. I was absolutely fascinated by it as a boy. The monorail was my personal model railway. I knew all the technical specifications. The timetables. The story of its origins. Everything.'

'And now?'

Waldemar shrugs his shoulders. 'Now it's just a railway. It goes from one end of Wuppertal to the other and back. Back and forth, back and forth. I prefer Zeppelins these days. If I had a Zeppelin I'd fly to Spain with you, Fraülein Dorly. For a start.'

❧

'Waldemar Velte talked to me enthusiastically, first about Wuppertal and then about Spain. Spain was a republic, he said. The land there was being shared out among poor peasant farmers and women had the vote. I told him he should get away from

Switzerland. I often got the feeling that he was suffering from wanderlust and homesickness at the same time.'

❧

Then the Minster clock strikes midnight. Dorly has to go home, her mother will be waiting up for her. Ramrod straight in her widow's weeds, she sits crocheting on the sofa for hour after hour, staring at the wall clock with red-rimmed eyes and determined not to go to bed before her daughter is between the sheets. It's always like this. Dorly has given up arguing long ago.

'Velte escorted me over Wettstein Bridge and along Rittergasse to Globus, where we said goodbye. He and his friend made a very favourable impression on me. They were polite and well dressed, had good manners and didn't behave in a pushy way – they certainly didn't get fresh with us. It wasn't a serious relationship as far as I was concerned. I liked them both, but Velte especially. He told me he first had to travel widely and see how his career developed. Later he would come back, and then we'd see. I suppose that by the end of that evening we loved each other platonically, as they say. I got the impression that Marie had fallen for Kurt Sandweg, not that she ever said as much to me.'

It is nearly one in the morning when Dorly quietly opens the living room door. Sure enough, her mother is sitting on the sofa crocheting a lace tablecloth. She doesn't look up when her daughter comes in. Dorly slips off her shoes, which are sodden inside and frozen outside, and massages her feet. They stopped aching long ago; the pain will return in a few minutes and make up for lost time when the warmth penetrates her bones.

'I told my mother that I'd spent the evening with two young men who had only introduced themselves by their first names because they had to suppress their surnames for political reasons. She expressed the suspicion that they were white slavers and forbade me to bring them home under any circumstances. Not to worry, I replied, they're leaving soon.'

7

It's getting even colder with the approach of Christmas. Thick ice floes are drifting down the Rhine, the seagulls perched on them hitching a ride to the north. Black smoke is rising from every chimney, and the stocks of coal in many a cellar will run out long before spring. Those who have money are now ordering fresh supplies. Others who still have some money left are hurriedly buying the last of their Christmas presents.

On the morning of 15 December, Sandweg and Velte collect *Grüss mir mein Hawaii* from Globus but also order a third record for the following day. There is no more talk of their leaving. That evening they wait for Dorly and Marie at the advertising pillar in Marktplatz. Kurt has opened the *National-Zeitung* and is studying the cinema programmes.

The Alhambra Cinema in the city centre is showing *Madame Butterfly* with Sylvia Sidney in the leading role and Cary Grant as Pinkerton. 'An enchanting series of scenes recounts the story of the life, love and death of the poor little geisha who, consumed with longing, takes the only way out by committing harakiri in accordance with the cruel custom of her forefathers.'

The Forum Cinema at Johanniter Bridge is showing *Was Frauen träumen,* a sparkling film comedy with Gustav Fröhlich and Nora Gregor. 'The fantastic story of a seductive, bewitchingly attractive kleptomaniac who steals only the finest jewellery. Whenever she seems about to be caught by the police, a mysterious man appears out of the blue and rescues her. The police are as much in the dark as the audience – until fate brutally tears the veil aside.'

Showing at the Morgarten Cinema is *Ladies of the Big House* with Sylvia Sidney and Gene Raymond. 'The best-looking couple in movies in a tremendous film. The story of a married couple who, unjustly condemned to death, courageously fight their way back to life and the paradise of love. Admission: 55 rappen.'

Also showing are *Devil and the Deep* with Gary Cooper, *Song of Songs* with Marlene Dietrich, and *King Kong* with Fay Wray.

Marie isn't against going – *Madame Butterfly* would be of particular interest to her. 'But Dorly simply didn't want to go to the cinema, so what were we to do?' They turned up their coat collars and went walking beside the Rhine again.

Ice floes have accumulated further downriver in the big bend beside the Lorelei. They collide with a deafening crash, splintering and rolling over and piling up into a bizarre Arctic landscape that stretches from bank to bank for ten kilometres. The Rhine has disappeared beneath thousands of tons of crepitating ice. Boys make it a test of courage to walk over the treacherous floes from one bank to the other, but Dorly, Marie, Waldemar and Kurt don't go to those lengths. In the Rhine Port, barges are firmly imprisoned in the ice. They will not resume their journey to Rotterdam until the thaw sets in. Bored seamen lounge around in Kaistrasse watching skaters glide out of the city and along the frozen riverbank, circle the floating dock, vanish behind the coal dump and reappear beside the loading bridge.

'Kurt Sandweg had brought some skates with him that evening. They were the kind you could clamp to your shoes, and he wanted to try them out in the harbour basin. Sandweg had also brought a pair for Marie Stifter, but she flatly refused to put them on, and besides, it would have been difficult to attach them to women's shoes. Sandweg had never skated before in his life, and he made a regular clown's act out of it. Occasionally, when he managed to go straight for several metres, he would stand up straight as a ramrod and yell triumphantly. But he would promptly begin to swerve and his ankles would bend over, his knees buckle, and the skates' leather insteps scrape the ice. Then he would fall over, laugh, and get up again at once. He made us laugh a great deal. I recall telling Velte that he and Sandweg were a comic couple, one a clown and the other a regular gravedigger. Velte was very shocked at this and asked me what I meant. I couldn't really tell him.'

8

Marie Stifter went for a walk with Kurt Sandweg, Waldemar Velte and Dorly Schupp on two successive nights, and each time she had to run to catch the last train, which was the 23:40 from Platform 7. On the second night she snapped off her left heel in the booking hall. She hobbled along the underpass and up the steps to the platform. The booking hall's wrought-iron roof was high and dark, the lighting dim and cold. The stationmaster's metallic loudspeaker voice reverberated around the spacious concourse. The platform was deserted. The guard had already closed the carriage doors and got in, but one door was still open near the top of the steps when Marie emerged from the underpass. Ernst Walder was standing there with one foot on the platform and one on the running board. He helped her to get in, and the train pulled out just as she flopped down on a seat in an empty compartment.

'Phew, that was close!'

'What happened to your shoe?'

'The heel snapped off.'

'Show me.'

Marie handed Ernst the shoe and the heel. Biting his lip, he closely examined both bits and held them up against each other. Five bent nails were protruding from the sole where the heel had been attached.

'You're out of breath. Run far?'

'All the way up Freie Strasse and along Elisabethenstrasse.'

'That's quite a way.' Ernst took the first of the five nails between his thumb and forefinger and tried to straighten it.

'Yes. Quite a way.'

'You had to run last night as well,' he said without looking up from the shoe. 'And you had someone with you.' Having straightened the first nail, he tackled the second.

'But … You mean you followed me?'

'You had someone with you again tonight. You needn't have sent him away outside the station.'

'You followed me?'

'I saw you and you saw me.'

'You *did* follow me!'

'We had a date and you stood me up.' The second nail had also been straightened. Ernst took hold of the third.

Marie shook her head. 'We had a date yesterday, not today.'

'We had a date, but you preferred to go for a walk with two men.'

'You *did* follow me!'

'You went for a walk with two men. You climbed into boats and put your arms round each other. You threw stones and climbed around on building sites and went skating – oh, goddammit, goddammit, goddammit!' Ernst had accidentally driven the fourth nail under his thumbnail. It started bleeding quite profusely.

'Stop swearing!' Marie took a white handkerchief from her handbag and wound it around his thumb. 'I can't stand swearing!' It was customary in the village for men to swear and women to scold them for it. The sexes complemented each other admirably in that respect at least.

'How hard it's bleeding!'

'You climbed into boats together and hugged each other. Goddammit, goddammit! Tonight and last night.'

'Stop swearing. You followed me! Hold your hand up, then it won't bleed so much. Fancy spying on me – I wouldn't have thought it of you!'

'Nor would I. I wouldn't have thought I needed to, either. You climbed into boats together and chucked stones around!' Ernst took the shoe in his uninjured right hand and tackled the fifth nail with his left.

'It's wrong of you to spy on me like that. Take care, you'll get blood all over my shoe.'

'I am taking care. Don't act so surprised, goddammit! You saw me.'

'What? Now stop swearing. I didn't see you. All that surprises me is the way you keep taking the name of the Lord in vain, considering you don't believe in Him.'

'What do you mean? I'm only swearing, that's all.' As a youth, Ernst Walder had affected an atheism he often liked to parade. In other respects he was just as much of a Catholic as Marie and everyone else in the village.

'You saw me,' he insisted. 'Down by the boats, while I was standing behind that tree. At the harbour too, beside the freight train. Goddammit! Goddammit! I saw you'd seen me.'

'Behind the tree? Beside the freight train? That's just not true! I never saw you!'

'I'll tell you something else: you only hugged him because you'd seen me watching you. You mightn't have gone for a walk at all if you hadn't seen me – if I hadn't been able to watch you.'

'That's not true! Take that back at once!' Marie had only feigned indignation hitherto because she knew he was in the right, strictly speaking, but now he was doing her an injustice and she was genuinely offended.

'There, done.' Ernst had inserted the five nails in the holes and pressed the heel firmly against the sole. 'It won't last for ever, but it'll do for now.'

'I didn't see you down by the river, or at the harbour! To think you were following me and spying on me! I really wouldn't have thought it –'

'Be quiet. There's only one thing I want to know: Do you plan to go on walking beside the Rhine?'

Marie didn't reply.

'You can suit yourself.'

Marie didn't reply.

'Either you go on walking beside the Rhine, or you don't go on walking beside the Rhine.'

'Fancy spying on me! Give me that shoe, or I'll ruin my stocking as well.'

'It's up to you. Either you'll go for more walks beside the Rhine, or you won't.'

'There's blood on my shoe!'

And so on and so forth.

Half an hour later the train finally pulled into the local town and Marie and Ernst alighted. They'd said everything to each other and repeated it so often that the two of them would have felt sick if they'd had to hear or say any of it again. Nothing new occurred to them either, so they fell silent, in one of these silences that could last a long time. It had happened before now in the village that two schoolboys started to ignore each other like this, and that they never exchanged another word until the first of them was lying in his coffin, grizzled, wrinkled and dead.

The last bus had gone long ago. Grumbling beneath their breath, Marie and Ernst set off through snow, ice and darkness for the village, which was five kilometres away – he ten or fifteen paces in the lead, she hobbling along behind in perpetual fear for her left shoe. According to my grandfather it held out until she got home; my grandmother disputed this as fiercely as she disputed all he said on principle. She insisted that she'd actually had to cover the last two kilometres with her left foot unshod at the expense of her stocking, toenails and entire foot. Furthermore, she said, she'd been confined to bed the next day with a raging cold and a high temperature.

9

Whether Marie Stifter really caught a cold that night, or whether she only pretended to have one in order to avoid choosing between two tall and good-looking but utterly different men, nobody knows. At all events, she shut herself up in her room for the next few days and remained in bed. She opened her door to no one apart from her mother, who brought her tea and porridge three times a day and emptied the chamber pot. She sent all visitors away, especially Ernst Walder, who called day after day with steadily mounting fury. He felt he was in the right and longed for Marie to finally show a smidgen of remorse, whereupon he would magnanimously be able to forget the whole business. Instead, she punished him for his implacability by cold-shouldering him.

Ernst was grimly determined to win this battle. On the fifth day he came bearing 13 long-stemmed red roses. He snorted in time to his steps with the bouquet held out in front of him like a dagger. The postmistress, with her feet stretched out into the front garden and her hands folded on her round stomach, was sitting on the bench beside the front door in the pale winter sunlight. Lying asleep on the bench beside her was Hasso, the Appenzeller Mountain Dog. It was lunchtime, as ever when Ernst paid his call, and lunchtime was when the postmaster had his snooze. Ernst avoided running into his future father-in-law if he could possibly do so, for the postmaster had a short fuse that could ignite at the slightest provocation. If he heard a rat rustling in a sack of oats while busy in the stable, for instance, he could reach into it quick as a flash, pluck the rat out, hold it up in front of his face, and squeeze and squeeze until the animal, having emitted spine-chilling, baby-like screams for minutes on end, ran out of breath and life in the postmaster's fist. Anyone who has heard a rat scream in mortal terror knows that no ordinary man is capable of such a thing, only the postmaster, which was why all the villagers steered clear of him. Now, however, he was having his lunchtime snooze, so the way was clear for Ernst Walder.

He came to a halt 20 paces from the postmistress. 'So it's you again!' she bellowed in the loud, guttural tones native to the Basel hinterland. Hasso twitched his ears and slept on. There was no risk that her cry would rouse the postmaster from his slumbers. When he was asleep, he was asleep.

'Yes, it's me again!' Ernst yelled back. Although he had attended a teaching seminar in the local town and learnt that yelling wasn't educationally essential, he could yell as loudly as anyone else in the village when he had to. This was one of those occasions.

'I brought some flowers!' he yelled, looking not at the postmistress but at the upstairs window on the right, which was open a crack.

'I told you, she's ill!' bellowed the postmistress. 'I told you yesterday, I told you the day before yesterday, and I told you the day before that!'

'I thought she mightn't be ill any more!'

'She still is, though!'

'They're red roses!' Ernst yelled up at the window, waving

the bouquet so hard that several petals fluttered to the ground. 'Thirteen of them! Imported! From the city!'

'Roses? In the middle of winter?' The postmistress sternly inspected the flowers from afar. 'You might have thought of bringing the poor lass something before! There's no point now she's ill!'

'I could take them up to her room!'

'What an idea! I told you yesterday and the day before yesterday and the day before that! You've treated the girl disgracefully!'

'Me? The girl? Treated her disgracefully?' Ernst Walder was dumbfounded by this unwarranted interpretation of recent events. In schoolmasterly fashion he raised his right hand – the one holding the bouquet – and prepared to deliver a speech. Then, seeing the postmistress's belligerently jutting chin, he capitulated and held out the bouquet.

'Here are the flowers! Could they at least be taken to her?!' He had meant it as a question, but everything sounds like an order when you yell. 'Or should I feed them to the cows?' He could have sworn that the curtains of the right-hand upstairs window had just twitched.

'Cows don't eat thorny stuff! Give 'em here!' The postmistress got to her feet and extended a fleshy arm. Ernst covered the 20 paces between them and handed her the bouquet, whereupon she turned without a word and climbed the steps to the front door.

'Will you take them to her right away?' he asked. His voice shook with anger and a thick blue vein stood out on his forehead.

'Yes!' bellowed the postmistress, and disappeared into the hallway. Hasso stayed where he was and went on sleeping.

'Right away?'

'Yes!'

'THEN WHILE YOU'RE ABOUT IT, ASK HER IF SHE'LL MARRY ME!' The front door closed, and a moment later the right-hand upstairs window shut with a loud bang. This dislodged a pane of glass, which fell out of its frame and smashed on the paving stones a hand's-breadth from Hasso, or so Grandfather assured me 46 years later, while we were pruning the bramble hedge. Grandmother vigorously disputed this too.

❧

At 9:30 am on 16 December, when Marie Stifter, without any excuse, failed to turn up for work for the first time, Globus's personnel manager phoned for a new temporary shop assistant. The new girl started work at 10:30, and Marie never again had a paid job, for the rest of her life.

❧

Bereft of Marie's company, Dorly Schupp was reluctant 'to keep the date with Sandweg and Velte, because it would have looked to me too much like an assignation. I made a point of calling Marie's home to ask if she was coming to Basel that evening. She didn't come to the phone herself, but got her mother to tell me she was ill and couldn't make it. However, since I didn't know which guesthouse Sandweg and Velte were staying at, I couldn't let them know. So I felt obliged to show up for our rendezvous beside the advertising pillar, at least for a few minutes. When I got there, though, Velte and I struck up an interesting conversation – about what, I can't recall, but I didn't want it to end. So we went for a walk as we had on previous nights, this time as a threesome instead of a foursome. It was snowing and very cold. Once again, our route took us over the Central Rhine Bridge to Lower Rheinweg, along Schaffhauser-Rheinweg and into Grenzacherstrasse, across the railway bridge to Sankt-Alban-Rheinweg, and from there up the steps to Wettstein Bridge and along Rittergasse to Globus, where we said goodbye.'

At lunchtime the next day Waldemar and Kurt collect their fourth record from Dorly and order a fifth. It is 17 December 1933, the fifth day of their acquaintanceship. On 18 December they buy yet another record and go for a walk that evening, likewise on the 19th, 20th, 21st, 22nd, 23rd, and so on throughout the holiday season and into January.

It must have been one night shortly before Christmas when Kurt Sandweg spotted an automatic photo booth at the entrance to the Rheinbrücke Department Store – a Photomaton, as the apparatus was then called. Dorly Schupp could not remember the precise date when questioned by the police later on.

'Fräulein Dorly, do let us take some souvenir photos!'

'By all means. Carry on.'

'No, with you! All three of us!'

'Many thanks, but no.'

'Oh, come on!'

'Good heavens no. I suppose you want me to pull faces and kiss you.'

'No, we'll take some souvenir photos! Three of each of us, then we'll each have a picture of ourselves and the other two.'

'I'd rather not.'

'We're leaving soon, Fräulein Dorly. It'll be a farewell gift.'

Dorly laughs and walks on past the Photomaton booth.

'But Fräulein Dorly!'

'Leave it, Kurt.' Sandweg makes to go after her, but Velte catches him by the elbow. 'Fräulein Dorly doesn't want to leave any traces – any evidence.' He says it in a low voice, but loud enough for her to hear.

Dorly pauses with her back to them.

'Isn't that right, Fraülein Dorly?' Waldemar Velte smiles at her back. 'A photograph is like something in writing. One has to be careful.'

Dorly loses her temper at this. She turns and plants her hands on her hips. 'I got really annoyed and told Velte he had no right to lecture me on being careful and mistrusting people; after all, they were the ones who'd concealed their full names from me, whereas I had never made any secret of mine. I even told them they were welcome to know all about my ancestors for six or seven generations back. Then Velte looked remorseful, begged my pardon, and asked if he and Sandweg could use the Photomaton booth. I had no objection to that.'

Kurt and Waldemar squeeze into the booth and insert one coin after another in the slot. There's a succession of flashes and the two of them pull the faces Dorly was expecting. The machine spits out the pictures that still repose in police and newspaper archives to this day: of one or both, with and without hats, with and without cigarettes in the corners of their mouths, smiling unaffectedly or frowning earnestly. Dorly Schupp: 'I know the men in the photographs well. I was on friendly terms with one of them. I myself possess three such photographs, which are almost identical to the ones in the possession of the police. The two Germans gave them to me at the Photomaton booth. If you've no objection, I'd like to keep the pictures as a souvenir.'

The Globus department store closes at four on Christmas Eve. Dorly, Waldemar and Kurt walk into town for once, not down to the Rhine. 'At Velte's suggestion, we walked up Freie Strasse from Marktplatz. When he noticed that a jeweller's shop on our right was still open, he paused and expressed a wish to buy me a gold ring as a token of his friendship. I refused it – I even had to get angry with him before he dropped the idea.'

'On Wednesday, 3 January 1934, when I met the pair in Marktplatz a little after 8:00 pm as usual, we talked for a while and they escorted me home. When saying goodbye, Velte said I mustn't be surprised if I didn't meet up with them in Marktplatz at 8:00 pm the following day, Thursday, 4 January 1934, because a business commitment might prevent them from coming. When I got to Marktplatz at 8:00 pm on Thursday, 4 January 1934, they weren't there. I didn't see them at all that night.'

10

Kurt and Waldemar really were away on business during the night of 4–5 January 1934; to be exact, in a blue Ford V8, a Model A with a black hood, licence number BS15750, whose legal owner had parked it in Belchenstrasse shortly before. Dorly Schupp couldn't believe this for a long time. 'I think it very unlikely that Sandweg and Velte stole a Ford. Sandweg always raved about them being the finest cars in the world, but Velte swore he would never sit in a Ford because Henry Ford had subsidised the Nazis' election campaign.'

The Ford makes its leisurely way south-west, past the railway station and on to the outskirts of the city. It passes the Sankt Jakob football stadium on the right, the Schweizerhalle chemical plant's jumble of pipework on the left, and then the black derricks of the salt works. Before long the road turns off into the gentle foothills of the Jura, and then there's nothing but hard-frozen cow pastures and bare cherry trees. Every few kilometres the car passes through darkened farming villages. Powder snow swirls red in the glow of the rear lights. Sleepy cattle low in their dark byres, weary farmhands sigh in their attics, farmers grind their teeth on the lower floors.

My grandfather could wax lyrical over the Ford V8. 'It was Henry Ford's last great feat of engineering: roomy, powerful, and technologically 20 years ahead of its time; 3.6 litre engine capacity, 65 horsepower, and a maximum speed of 140 kilometres per hour. Fabulous. You shouldn't leave an apricot tree's fruitwood too long, Max.'

࿐

After 20 kilometres the car turns off and comes to a stop beside the road. It's just before 11:00 pm. The engine falls silent, the headlights go out. Visible in the background are the dark roofs of a village, and this side of them, almost illegible in the gloom, is a sign reading 'Sissach'. Two valleys further to the west, Marie Stifter and Ernst Walder are lying resentfully in their beds.

The car's roof light goes on for a minute or two, then darkness returns. From time to time the headlights of passing cars illuminate the Ford's interior, and Sandweg and Velte duck down below the dashboard. The engine cools, the exhaust pipe ticks. Once, the passenger winds down the side window and tosses out the piece of bacon rind and eight fig stalks the police will discover the next day. Silence falls.

The village roosters start crowing even before dawn. While farmhands are mucking out the stables, maids are lighting stoves and peasants bringing milk to the dairies, the blue Ford drives back to Basel. Half an hour later the car attracts the attention of a tram driver because the driver clearly doesn't know his way around. He will tell the police later that the car turned off to Aeschenvorstadt from Dufourstrasse at 7:52 am. 7:52 precisely? The tram driver is offended. He crosses Aeschenplatz at precisely 7:52 every morning in conformity with the timetable, that's why he knows the exact time. What's more, a second occupant of the Ford showed his pale face and green eyes in the rear window. Green eyes? Could he have seen their colour at that range and through two panes of glass? The tram driver again takes umbrage. 'If I saw green eyes, I saw green eyes.'

❧

There are 62 banks in Basel on 15 January 1934. They all open for business on the dot of 8:00 am. When the bells of the Minster strike eight, 62 junior bank clerks busy themselves with keys at their main entrances throughout the city. Unlocking the door in the morning is the junior clerk's job; locking it in the evening, an incomparably more responsible task, is that of the manager.

At the Wever Bank in Elisabethenstrasse, 18-year-old junior bank clerk Werner Siegrist performs the duty he has carried out since the start of his third probationary year, then brings the key back to Jacques Beutter, the authorised signatory and head cashier.

'Thanks, Siegrist. Haitz, you can go and fetch the mail now.'

Now in his second probationary year, Wilhelm Haitz is responsible for running errands to the main post office. Siegrist has that job behind him. He sits down at his desk, removes the dust cover from his Underwood, and proceeds to type out extracts from lists of stocks and shares. Haitz takes the handcart and sets off.

Wilhelm Haitz enjoys these excursions to the main post office, which he undertakes three times a day. They give him three half-hour doses of freedom and fresh air; three opportunities to eye the legs of the office girls who throng the main post office at all times of day; three chances to study the cinema posters in passing, smoke a surreptitious cigarette, and gossip with junior clerks from the Bankverein and the Kreditanstalt. It should be added that going is nicer than coming back. Although the route is the same, the post office is downhill and the handcart is empty. In summer the return trip can bring you out in a sweat when the cart is overflowing, and the uphill trek up Freie Strasse and along Elisabethenstrasse, almost as far as the Elisabethen Park, seems interminable. It's alright in July, when business is slack, incoming mail meagre, and the cart half empty. But in June and the second half of August! As so often in life, it ought to be the other way round: the bank should be down below and the post office up above. Then you could pull the empty handcart uphill with ease and simply coast downhill when it's full. Or you should be able to tilt the whole area as required: walk downhill to the post office, tilt the terrain in the other direction, and walk downhill to the bank. That would have been particularly practical during the heavy snowfalls two winters ago, when Freie Strasse was one big piste.

So Wilhelm Haitz goes his way daydreaming, empties the post box, collects the registered letters and parcels from the counter, and is back at the Wever Bank by 8:40 am. Parked on the pavement in the middle of the no-waiting area is a blue Ford with its engine idling and no one behind the wheel. At that moment, a young man comes running out of the bank wearing a grey-green overcoat and motoring goggles with dark yellow lenses. Swiftly, he gets in on the driver's side, depresses the clutch, engages first gear, and releases the handbrake. Then another man emerges from the bank. The second man gets in and climbs on to the back seat. Strange, thinks Haitz. In the cinema this would be a bank raid, no doubt about it. He stares after the Ford as it turns left into De-Wette-Strasse and disappears from view.

Little Haitz enters Wever's banking hall. There he sees his boss Jacques Beutter and head cashier Arnold Kaufmann slumped in their swivel chairs, streaming with blood. Beutter's swivel chair rolls backwards and rotates. The cashier loses his grip and slides slowly under his desk. Haitz shakes his head. He has warned his boss more than once that the swivel chairs have the wrong kind of castors. These are designed for carpeted floors, not lino, on which they roll far too easily. This can be dangerous. Haitz learnt this at the polytechnic, where he was issued with a leaflet from the Accident Insurance Institute. He passed this on to his superiors, but nobody listens to a probationer in his second year. Such are the things that go through little Haitz's mind, and he describes them in detail to the police shortly afterwards.

In the back room, junior clerk Siegrist is shouting 'Bank raid! Bank raid! Bank raid!' into the telephone receiver. The police get there seven minutes later, and Siegrist gives them as detailed and accurate an account as he can.

'This morning, around 9:35 …'

9:35? It's not even nine o'clock yet.

He can't be specific about the time, but two unknown, youngish men entered the banking hall by the front entrance when no one was there apart from Beutter, Kaufmann and himself. These unknown men went over to the two counters, one to each. At the same moment there was a loud cry of 'Hands up!' Because the two unknown men were levelling pistols at them and holding them at bay, he, Siegrist, had got to his feet. To the best of his recollection, Beutter and Kaufmann had done the same. After a few seconds, shots had rung out – five or six in all, he believed. On impulse, he had suddenly backed away from his desk and into the passage leading to the rear of the bank. He didn't know if any shots had been fired at him. In any event, he hadn't been hit. It was possible that he had fled before the first shot was fired.

An ambulance arrives soon after the police. Beutter and Kaufmann are lifted on to stretchers and carried out. They say a few words to the police before losing consciousness.

That morning the city is swarming with policemen who, on the strength of some very vague particulars, are looking for the bank robbers. Every few minutes, handcuffs click somewhere and they lead away another fellow unlucky enough to be fairly young and quite tall or quite short or in the company of another young man who is likewise quite tall or quite short. All the frontier posts are on the alert and all the railway stations under close surveillance.

At ten o'clock a police patrol finds the blue Ford V8 in Sankt-Alban-Rheinweg, where Waldemar and Kurt so often went walking with Dorly. Lying on the back seat is an empty cash bowl. According to the police report, the robbers' haul comprises '228 Swiss francs 27 rappen, 103 French francs 45 centimes, 119 Reichsmarks 83 pfennigs, also 8 silver Zeppelin memorial coins the size of an old 5 franc piece, dated 1929 and inscribed "Round-the-World Flight, August 1929" (value 6 francs 95 rappen each), and a gold coin of exactly the same description, market value 125 francs.'

❧

Ernst Walder paid no more visits to the post office after his appearance with the 13 red roses. Both before and after the

Christmas holidays, he taught at the primary school as usual, conducted the rehearsals of the male voice choir as usual, and attended Party and parish meetings and football and athletics club training sessions as usual, but he steered well clear of the post office and the *Zur Traube* restaurant. And Marie Stifter? She obdurately kept to her room for as long as three weeks and never showed her face on Christmas Eve, Christmas Day, or at New Year's.

On the evening of 4 January, Postmaster Stifter decided that enough was enough. He dug his Sunday suit out of the wardrobe, lit a cigarette, and strode through the village to have a word with ex-schoolmaster Walder. After all, he said, Ernst had loudly requested his Marie's hand in marriage outside the post office, so what was going on? The old schoolmaster wagged his head. Diplomatically, he said that, to the best of his knowledge, there had been no formal proposal and he must first consult Walder Junior. The postmaster's response was to yell, 'Come off it, don't talk nonsense! The whole village heard your boy yelling outside my house!' He started to turn purple, so the old schoolmaster quickly caved in. They soon agreed on the financial details. The wedding day was fixed for the third Saturday after Easter. It was also agreed that Ernst would pay a courtesy visit to the post office at lunchtime the next day, and that he would again bring some roses – 27 this time, not 13 – as a mark of atonement. In return, Marie was instructed to open her window and give Ernst a friendly wave as soon as he came within 20 paces. If possible, she should also blow him a kiss. Then the two of them would go for a walk. Meantime, the postmaster and postmistress would have their siesta and not show their faces.

Although Marie couldn't bring herself to blow Ernst a kiss,

everything passed off as agreed in other respects. While a feverish manhunt for two bank robbers was in progress in Basel, Marie and Ernst trudged across field and meadow, their hips, elbows and umbrellas colliding, and talked for the sake of it. Each was grimly determined to worst the other, to put him or her in the wrong. It was a contest in which the loser would be the first to display resentment and pick the quarrel that was so long overdue. And because neither was prepared to give way at any price, their walk ended in a kiss – and a clash of teeth – behind the postmaster's house. From that moment on, they were regarded as officially betrothed.

In the Wever Bank's banking hall, measurements and photographs are taken, interviews conducted and recorded in shorthand, money counted and diagrams drawn. Junior clerk Werner Siegrist tells all he knows again and again. 'The perpetrators had undoubtedly reconnoitred Wever & Co's banking hall prior to the raid. This they had done by changing foreign currency or making enquiries about foreign exchange rates. But they were not accurately informed, or they would have taken not the silver but the paper money in the next drawer, which amounted to several thousand francs. Nothing was removed from the drawer containing the paper money even though it was unlocked.'

Shortly before 11:00 am, Jacques Beutter and Arnold Kaufmann undergo surgery in Basel's Bürgerspital. Police records state that Beutter had two bullet wounds. 'One of the projectiles had pierced his buttock; the other had entered beneath his right arm and passed through the whole of his upper body, fatally injuring his windpipe and gullet. Young Kaufmann, on the other hand, had sustained a single transverse shot through the head.' Beutter dies on the operating table, Kaufmann in intensive care 12 hours later.

11

The morning edition of Basel's *National-Zeitung* comes out just before 11:00 am. A paperboy's voice rings out across Marktplatz: 'Bank raid in Elisabethenstrasse!' A young woman with a big basket of vegetables in each hand buys three copies from him. It's Johanna Furrer, a landlady who runs a small guesthouse in Herbergstrasse. She carries her baskets home and sees to lunch, which is simmering on the stove. There's just time for her to do the room occupied by the two Germans who always sleep so late and spend whole afternoons playing gramophone records.

'When I went in, the Germans were standing there in their trousers and vests, smoking cigarettes. I asked them if they'd heard what had happened that morning. "No, what?" said the taller of the two, so I told them about the bank raid that had taken place. They both expressed their abhorrence of the crime and the criminals. While in their room I noticed two large parcels tied up in brown paper that hadn't been there the evening before. At midday the two Germans appeared in the dining room and had lunch with my other boarders. Those present argued fiercely about the bank raid during the meal. They did not take part in the conversation, however, but talked only to each other.'

The Germans have disappeared by the time Johanna Furrer

brings in the coffee. The key to their room is hanging on the board. She can't get those parcels out of her head. Although tied up in a slipshod fashion, they were lying very prominently in the middle of the room. She takes the key and goes upstairs. 'The parcels weren't lying on the floor or the table or on either of the two chairs. All that was in the wardrobe were two suitcases and the gramophone case, but they were all locked, so I can't say if the parcels contained raincoats. They might have, from the size, but I never saw the two Germans wearing raincoats, only tweed overcoats. What I found striking about the pair was that they were always together. They only asked for one house key, even when they checked in, because they were always in each other's company. It was also strange that they seldom turned the light on in their room, even at night, and that they were always playing music on their gramophone, tangos mostly. If they were German songs, one of them would sometimes sing along with them. The tall one, I think it was.'

Meanwhile, the owner of the blue Ford has reported its theft to city police headquarters. He gets his car back after forensics have examined it for evidence, the photographer has taken his pictures, and the mechanic has repaired the ignition lock, but the following items are missing:

'1 ignition key No. 1013 A; 3 tubes of "Sibo" shaving cream; 2 pairs of horn-rimmed glasses, one with circular dark yellow lenses, the other with green; 1 cardboard glasses case inscribed "Frei".'

Also at the same time, in Globus's gramophone records department, the red lift door opens and the bell pings. Kurt and Waldemar emerge. Dorly is surprised when neither of them says hello. Kurt promptly disappears behind the nearest shelf unit and peers around the shop. 'I made some jocular remark to the effect that the two Germans were my best customers, and I'd probably soon be promoted to senior assistant on the strength of my excellent sales figures. Then Velte came over to me looking even more sombre than usual. He informed me that the letter they'd been expecting had finally arrived. They would have to travel on to Spain, and from there possibly overland to India. Couldn't I knock off a little earlier, so we had time to say goodbye? They would then tell me their full names. They would even show me their passports if I wanted.'

❧

Early that afternoon, Wilhelm Sperisen, proprietor of the eponymous Kleinbasel gunsmith's, reported the theft of two 7.65 mm automatic pistols to Lohnhof police station. 'Shortly before midday yesterday, two young men entered my shop. One of them distracted me with a lot of friendly small talk while the other helped himself to the goods unobserved. I didn't originally mean to report the theft because I assumed the thieves would never be caught, so reporting it would be more trouble than it was worth. After today's bank raid, however, I realised that the matter might be important to the police.'

❧

Bank Clerk Werner Siegrist spends the evening of the raid at

CID headquarters. He is the only eyewitness. For hours on end, dozens of suspects – young men of tall, medium and really diminutive stature – are paraded for his inspection, but none of them resembles either of the perpetrators. Little Haitz, by contrast, is lucky enough not to be needed by the police because he saw nothing, or as good as nothing. He's sitting in a cinema, watching *King Kong* for the seventh time.

༄

Daily report by Detective Superintendent Hoffmann, head of Team 4: 'Shots were undoubtedly fired by both suspects. What is certain is that the taller suspect fired a shot at junior bank clerk Siegrist when the latter fled, but failed to hit him. Being unable to continue firing at Siegrist after the latter's disappearance, it seems he went at once to the other counter and there fired one or two more shots at Beutter and Kaufmann. His accomplice must also have fired at least three shots at the above-named.'

༄

After closing time, Dorly, Waldemar and Kurt go for a walk along the Rhine for the last time. It isn't as cold as it was in December. The north wind from Siberia has retreated northwards; the familiar nor'wester is blowing moist sea air from the British Isles, and there's a smell of wet wool. The ice on the Rhine is becoming thinner, breaking up and drifting towards the North Sea. Barges hoot, impatient to be on their way, and the crews listen apprehensively to the throb of their diesel engines to see if the frost has done any damage. Dorly,

Waldemar and Kurt walk across the Central Bridge; Dorly and Waldemar side by side as usual, Kurt some way ahead or behind or on a level with them. They carry straight on until the coppery green belfry of St Clare's Church looms up at the end of Greifengasse.

'Velte had often suggested that the three of us should visit a church, but Sandweg and I had always declined to. This time he refused to back down, however, so we went into St Clare's. We all sat down in silence, side by side in the front pew on the right of the centre aisle. I can't say if Sandweg and Velte prayed; we didn't speak, anyway. Velte buried his face in his hands, rocked back and forth, and seemed completely self-absorbed, whereas Sandweg and I just waited until we'd had enough. After about half an hour, Sandweg couldn't stand it any longer and insisted on going, but Velte took a lot of persuading to leave. Back outside at last, we walked back over the Central Bridge and up Freie Strasse to the Central Station, where Sandweg jotted down departure times for the South of France. Then they escorted me home. On the way I repeated my previous request to be told their full names. They had earlier refused to show me their passports on all kinds of pretexts. This time I insisted, saying that one couldn't really know a person or thing unless one could call it by its real name. This impressed Velte in particular, and eventually, outside our house, the two of them consented to show me their passports. I memorised their names, hometowns and dates of birth because I'd grown fond of them both. This is why I was able to give their exact particulars at my first police interview without having written them down.

'The following day we met by arrangement at 1:00 pm in Marktplatz. The two of them took me to Pension Furrer, saying that they had to collect something. I declined their request to accompany them up to their room and waited outside the guesthouse. When they rejoined me Sandweg was carrying two suitcases and Velte a holdall and the portable gramophone. At the station Sandweg brought some tickets but didn't show me them and said they were travelling to Marseille via Pontarlier/Lyon. Velte said he would write from Marseille to tell me where their adventures would take them after that.

'They were scheduled to leave at 2:50 that afternoon, but we were all so engrossed in conversation that we missed the train and remained in the second-class waiting room until the next one left at 4:05. Then the two of them boarded the train on Platform 4 and left by way of Delémont. I felt so upset, I went straight home and up to my room without saying hello to my mother. I was firmly convinced that I would never see Sandweg and Velte again.'

12

On 8 January 1934, Waldemar sends Dorly a picture postcard from Lyon:

'Dear Dorly, in great haste, warmest regards from Lyon from your friend Waldemar. Just on the train to Marseille. Letter follows. My friend Kurt also sends warmest regards.'

At Globus, the Christmas rush is over; now is the time for exchanges. Dorly takes receipt of the gramophone records that find their way back to her: the big Wagner album which a blushing schoolboy swaps for three really awful jazz records; the Chopin preludes which a girl surrenders in favour of some lace underwear; George Gershwin's *Rhapsody in Blue,* which an elderly gentleman exchanges for Bach's *Goldberg Variations.* It may happen that the girl is the daughter of the elderly gentleman and the schoolboy is her brother, and that all three have given each other gramophone records for Christmas. They may miss one another by only a few minutes, thereby sparing themselves an embarrassing family encounter. Dorly preserves a discreet silence as she listens to their mumbled falsehoods, works out price differences and delivery dates, makes out credit notes and ties up parcels; and after closing time she leaves the shop by the staff exit and walks past the advertising pillar, where nobody is waiting for her. The nights at home are long. Her mother sits over her sewing for hour after hour and the ticking of the wall clock is the only sound.

On 12 January a letter arrives from the South of France. Three weeks later, Dorly gives it to a reporter from the *National-Zeitung* to stop him pestering her:

'Marseille, 10 January 1934. Dear Dorly, we're back in Marseille! Our journey is and remains an ill-starred venture. At the Spanish frontier a gold-braided, operetta-esque customs officer refused to let us through because our papers weren't to his taste. So we had to turn round and make our way back through this operetta-esque southern French countryside with its palm trees, vineyards, luxury hotels and wild horses, which looks exactly like a German old age pensioner's idea of the South of France.

'So we're back in Marseilles. At least I'm a little closer to Basel and you, dear Dorly. At this moment Kurt is down at the harbour, looking at ships. He likes ships. I'm writing to you here on the sun terrace of a coffee house, and it's almost like spring already. We'll now have to think of what to do next – make another attempt to get into Spain, or opt for another route? I've really lost my desire for travel lately. After all, why bother? All this hassle with passports and visas and transit permits and timetables, this eternal money changing – marks into French francs, French francs into Swiss francs, Swiss francs back into French francs, francs into pesetas, pesetas into francs. It goes on forever, and what's the upshot? You realise that the world is one big fortress. A prison, an inescapable Alcatraz. You'd need a moon rocket at your disposal. From that point of view, a Zeppelin's not much better than a monorail.

'Anyone richer than Kurt and I, or smarter and more reckless, might make it to Spain and even further, but it would still be an escape from one prison cell into another, from prison cell France to prison cell Spain, and after that would inevitably come the next cell, Morocco, Libya, Egypt, India, and so on. I realise that now. If you really wanted to escape and not simply run from one cell into the next, you'd have to go further afield, much further – to the last blank spaces on the map. There are always some somewhere, but it's a peculiarity of blank spaces that you can't get to them. Otherwise they wouldn't be blank.

'Dear Dorly, everyone talks about America. But what would I do there? Recently I read in the newspaper about the so-called Court Restaurants in Chicago, where members of the upper crust titillate themselves by eating the same supper as someone due to be executed in the same building at the same time. Should a place where such things happen be the goal of my dreams? Tell me, Dorly, do you understand me? Yes, you do, I'm quite sure.

'Perhaps Kurt and I should meekly go home to Wuppertal and report to the Labour Service. What do you think? We could put up with it for a while. We'd simply have to keep our eyes, ears and mouths shut, do the lottery on Fridays, and worry about nothing but ourselves. In a few months' time we would find technicians' jobs in a steel or coal concern. We would have to join the obligatory Nazi industrial technicians' association, but we could afford a three-room flat. Then you could join us, and the three of us would live together. What do you think, Dorly? There are department stores in Wuppertal too, you know. You'd be bound to find a job.

'But no, that's not on, that's nonsense. There's a divine order of things we can't escape – there must be! Life, nonsensical?

Meaningless? No, never! It does have meaning! We must fight on, liberate ourselves. And if God wills it, you and I will soon be reunited, wherever and under whatever circumstances. *If fate should smile on me, I'll bless the day, but if it turns its back, I'll simply say: Be comforting and hold me close, in your sweet hands I'll find repose.* Your friend, Waldemar.'

ꕥ

Sitting in Basel's CID headquarters is a man with huge paws and powerful jaw muscles. 'I, Karl Kaufmann-Langenegger, born 1896, fitter, resident of Füllinsdorf, Baselland, hereby offer a reward of 1000 francs for information leading to the arrest of the guilty parties. The man murdered in the Wever Bank, Arnold Kaufmann, was my brother. Read and signed at Basel, 12 January 1934. Karl Kaufmann.'

ꕥ

From the *Schweizerischer Polizeianzeiger,* or police gazette, Bern: 'It seems from the attendant circumstances of the Stuttgart and Basel bank raids that the two are connected, although existing descriptions of the suspects differ in important respects. Moreover, ballistics experts have ascertained that all the shots in Stuttgart came from one weapon, whereas in Basel shots were fired from two different weapons and the Stuttgart and Basel pistols are not identical. All three weapons are automatic pistols, calibre 7.65 mm, but their make cannot be established for want of sufficient characteristics. It can, however, be stated that those involved are two youngish men, one of whom is somewhat taller than the other, that both move with speed and agility, and that they are determined to stop at nothing.

'If the assumption that a connection exists between Stuttgart and Basel is correct, the robbers can soon be expected to reappear under similar circumstances in other cities, given that their haul in Basel amounted to only about 350 francs in silver. It is requested that special attention be paid to these incidents, and that any relevant information be transmitted to CID Stuttgart and Basel without delay. Substantial rewards for clearing up the crimes have been posted in both cases.'

Junior Bank Clerk Werner Siegrist has a hard time in the days following the bank raid. Day and night, police sidecar motorcycles pull up outside his parents' house, ready to collect him for identity parades. He is taken away from his work and roused from sleep almost nightly. He is losing his appetite, suffering from insomnia and depression. One night, however, when the Siegrist family is at supper in the kitchen and the doorbell rings yet again, Siegrist Senior deliberately folds his napkin like the conscientious railwayman he is, puts it down on the table, and says: 'Right, that's it. They're driving the boy insane.' He goes to the door and tells the policeman to push off, and when the latter threatens him, he raises his voice, brandishes his fist, and sends him packing. Next morning, Junior Bank Clerk Siegrist leaves by train for a rest cure in Montreux, where the railwayman's union owns a hotel. The Wever Bank foots the bill.

Saturday, 13 January 1934. Dorly has had to cut down on her overtime and can't go to work. This doesn't suit her, because the time passes more quickly at Globus than it does at home with her mother. In three hours' time it will be exactly one week since Kurt Sandweg and Waldemar Velte left. The electric bell in the passage rings. Dorly and her mother don't possess a telephone of their own, but they're able to use that of the Herzog family on the third floor in return for a small charge. Dorly recently had the bell installed in the passage to save the Herzogs from having to come downstairs to summon them to the phone.

Dorly climbs the stairs. She doesn't get many phone calls, and they're usually from workmates wanting her to give up a free day for them. This time, however, it's Waldemar on the line. 'Velte told me they were back in Basel. Their second attempt to enter Spain had also failed, he said, because they didn't have any visas and would have to obtain those in Berlin. We arranged to meet at 2:00 pm at Brausebad, and we did. Then we went for a walk as usual.'

13

'Where's the cemetery in Basel, Fräulein Dorly?'

'There are several. Some very famous people are buried in the Minster.'

'What about ordinary people?'

'In the Hörnli Cemetery, but that's a long way off. It's down-river, near the German frontier.'

'Shall we go there?'

'No, we won't!' Kurt Sandweg swung round and raised his hand like a traffic policeman. 'We won't, will we, Fraülein Dorly?'

❧

'It was the first time I'd seen Sandweg flare up like that. However, since Velte couldn't be dissuaded from wanting to visit the Hörnli Cemetery, I took them there. We spent a long time walking between the rows of graves – the Hörnli is the biggest and most modern cemetery in Switzerland, after all. It struck me that Sandweg seemed uncharacteristically uneasy, whereas Velte was excited and in high spirits. He showed great interest in all kinds of tombstones and paused and read Sandweg and me the inscriptions on them. He found many of them so amusing, he couldn't help laughing and was almost irrepressible. At one stage he said he'd like to be buried in the Hörnli; then he would always be near me.'

❧

On 16 January 1934, Bonnie Parker and Clyde Barrow use machine guns to spring the gangsters Ray Hamilton and Henry Methvin from Eastham Prison Farm, Texas. In the process, Clyde shoots and kills a guard who tries to prevent their getaway.

❧

Kurt and Waldemar resume their Basel routine. At lunchtime they visit Dorly in Globus and buy a gramophone record; the afternoons they spend in their room, playing one record after another on the portable gramophone; when darkness falls they have an early evening meal at the *Markthalle,* their favourite restaurant near the Central Station. At closing time they wait for Dorly beside the advertising pillar in Marktplatz, then go for a walk beside the Rhine. This happens on Monday, Tuesday, Wednesday and Thursday. They follow the same routine on Friday as well – but only until 6:23 pm.

At that time, Detective Corporal Hans Maritz is on plain-clothes duty at the Central Station. He has joined the longest queue in front of the ticket office in order to keep a surreptitious eye on two young men, one somewhat taller than the other and both looking as if they would 'stop at nothing'. Maritz is regarded as 'one of Basel's finest detectives, thanks to his nose for trouble', as Pastor Hans Baur will put it during the funeral ceremony at the Hörnli a week later. An observant onlooker would be struck by the fact that Maritz is the only person in the booking hall wearing an old-fashioned wing collar. A 45-year-old married man without children, Maritz is the eldest son of a fitter employed by the Basel gasworks, a policeman of over 20 years' standing, and president of the police marksmen's club. He advances steadily up the queue. When he gets to the counter and it's his turn, he peels off and goes over to the kiosk, where he notices '… two suspicious individuals who could have fitted the description of the Wever bank raiders, the taller of whom was buying a bar of chocolate. In the course of a subsequent identity check, I ascertained that they were German nationals and took them to the station police post for questioning. However, since they were able to identify themselves properly and produce a satisfactory reason for being in Basel (a business trip on behalf of the building trade), I had no occasion to make further inquiries.'

❧

It's pouring with rain in Marktplatz. Dorly, sheltering beneath her umbrella, has been waiting beside the advertising pillar for the past ten minutes. At last, Kurt and Waldemar come dashing across the square with their coat tails flying.

'Fraülein Dorly! Thank goodness you're still here!'

❧

'Both extremely agitated, they explained that they'd been detained by the police at the Central Station, taken to the police post, and made to show their passports. Everything was found to be in order and they'd been released unscathed, but it had been an embarrassing and unpleasant business. I can confirm that they had some chocolate with them that evening. Sandweg offered me some, but I declined because I thoroughly dislike sweet things. If I remember correctly, it was a bar of Lindt nut chocolate in a blue and white wrapper. Velte said they had to go to Berlin as soon as possible to get their visas for another trip to Spain, if possible that night or early the next morning.'

❧

The trains to Germany leave from Baden Station on the city's northern outskirts, not from the Central Station. Waldemar and Kurt squeeze in under Dorly's umbrella to the left and right of her. They cross the Rhine by the Central Bridge, walk past St Clare's Church and go straight on to Baden Station. Waldemar and Dorly sit quietly on a bench beneath the huge, vaulted roof of the booking hall while Kurt busily notes down departure times, buys tickets and food for the journey, and changes money. Their train leaves at 8:45 the next morning.

'I was surprised when Sandweg bought tickets to Cologne because it isn't, as far as I know, on the route to Berlin. When I questioned Velte about this, he told me they had to go home first because they'd almost run out of money and he had to report to his father. Because it was raining so hard, we remained in the entrance hall at Baden Station for over two hours. Later we went to the guesthouse at 83 Sperrstrasse, where I went up to their room with them for the first and only time. They packed their suitcases, and after spending about 20 minutes in the room, we left. The two of them set out to escort me home, but at Schifflände Kurt Sandweg took his leave, pleading the downpour. Velte walked on with me. He wouldn't take a tram. We never took a tram, always walked in rain or snow, however cold it was. Velte couldn't help crying when we said goodbye outside the door of our house at 23 Palmenstrasse, and I made some consoling remarks designed to cheer him up. We didn't embrace, even on this occasion, nor did Velte ever demand anything of the kind. I offered him my umbrella but he refused it, saying he wouldn't be able to return it. I advised him to take it with him and leave it at the guesthouse, whence I would collect it in due course. Which he did.'

14

The rain had stopped at dawn and mist rises from the drains. A fat, bowler-hatted man armed with an umbrella is panting along the streets of Kleinbasel preceded by a skinny policeman in uniform. They are Detective Corporal Jakob Vollenweider and Constable Alfred Nafzger, who are going from hotel to hotel and guesthouse to guesthouse in search of the two bank robbers. Vollenweider is finding it hard to keep up with Nafzger. He is 20 years older and 100 pounds heavier, has chalked up 23 more years' service, and is suffering from a gastric ulcer likely to earn him premature retirement in a year or two. Nafzger, by contrast, is still on the threshold of his career. Originally a waiter by training, he has taken only four years to become chairman of the Basel Police Federation. However, he made himself unpopular with his colleagues during the latest wage negotiations by displaying too much sympathy for the employers' side.

Every available policeman has been on full-time duty since the raid on the Wever Bank. All hotels are being systematically checked, and railway stations, customs posts and *bureaux de change* are under constant surveillance. Hundreds of men are being questioned for hours or even days because they are young or unemployed or somewhat shorter or taller than someone else. The police are doing their best, but the first readers' letters are appearing in the press:

'Quo vadis, Basel police? The Wever bank robbers have been promenading through our city and enjoying themselves on their blood money for over two weeks. And what are our police doing? Dishing out parking tickets to innocent citizens.'

The communist and social democratic papers accuse the police of beating up proletarian demonstrators but letting real murderers and robbers go. The bourgeois papers call for stricter laws relating to foreigners, tougher penalties for crimes against property, and arms for the police. This throws a scare into the politicians, with the result that the Grand Council is being bombarded with interpellations, claims and motions. This, in turn, alarms Police Commissioner Carl Ludwig, who fears for his chances of re-election. He demands that his men arrest the bank robbers soonest.

This morning, 20 January 1934, Detective Corporal Vollenweider and Constable Nafzger have already checked on a guesthouse in Haltingerstrasse. They now make their way to Hedwig Vetter's nearby guesthouse at 83 Sperrstrasse – 'a pretty shady establishment', as even the social democratic *Arbeiter-Zeitung* will call it. The police have picked up ten suspicious individuals there in the last week alone.

'My relations with the police aren't good,' Hedwig Vetter will state. 'I actually believe they hate me. I've been running my guesthouse for twenty years; until six years ago I sometimes had a policeman boarding with me, but not since then.' She has already been penalised three times for failing to notify the police of her guests.

Reluctantly, the landlady opens her door to the policemen. She conducts Vollenweider and Nafzger upstairs in her dressing gown and curlers. 'I wanted to take the policemen first to Room Number 2, where the two Germans – my classiest boarders – were staying.' But the policemen proceed methodically and begin by knocking on the door of Room Number 1. It is opened by Friedrich Seitz, a 52-year-old German from Baden. An actor and travelling salesman of no fixed abode, Seitz has a razor in his hand and shaving foam all over his face. Hedwig Vetter: 'Detective Vollenweider asked Seitz who he was, and Seitz replied, "I'm Fritz Seitz." Then Vollenweider checked his "Wanted" file and said to Seitz, "In that case, you'll have to come down to the station."'

Seitz is known to the police. Most recently, he was arrested in Zurich on 30 October and expelled from the country for the sixth time. He has a girlfriend named Lina Hottinger in Zurich's Kuttelgasse who is keen to marry him, and it's because of her that he keeps coming back.

Detective Corporal Vollenweider moves on to Room Number 2. Constable Nafzger continues to stand in Seitz's doorway to prevent him from decamping. Vollenweider knocks, knocks again and again and calls: 'Police! Open up at once!'

The door opens at last. Seated on the nearer of the two beds is a tall young man wearing only a pair of trousers. He is just doing up his shoelaces. Standing beside the door, also half dressed, is a short young man with green eyes. Vollenweider enters and asks for their papers. The tall man reaches into the breast pocket of his jacket, which is draped over the back of a chair. While Nafzger is outside in the passage, ensuring that Seitz doesn't escape, Vollenweider enquires the two men's occupation: civil engineers. Where have they come from? Marseille. Then Vollenweider sees the taller man reaching stealthily for the right-hand outside pocket of his coat. The detective lunges at him, shouting: 'What – so you've got a gun!', pushes him back on the bed, and hurls himself on top of him. Alarmed by the sudden commotion, landlady Hedwig Vetter dashes out of the room. By contrast, Constable Nafzger comes to Vollenweider's aid and dashes in. This, however, is a mistake. For one thing, actor and travelling salesman Friedrich Seitz is now free to make off; for another, on entering the room Nafzger has presented his back to the second suspect, who is standing beside the door. This violates a basic rule governing spot checks: never take your eyes off a suspect individual. Waldemar Velte fires three shots at Nafzger, hitting him in the head, back and upper thigh. The policeman topples backwards, past the landlady and down the stairs, while Velte looses off his remaining rounds at Vollenweider's broad back.

Vollenweider is killed instantly, pinning Sandweg to the bed beneath his bulk. The latter cannot get up until Velte pushes the corpse off him. The detective corporal's head hits the wall, denting his bowler hat. His legs, which are hanging over the edge of the bed and out into the room, twitch once or twice.

Constable Nafzger has reached the street. His mouth is filling up with blood and everything is going black before his eyes. On the corner of Hammerstrasse stands an inn named *Zum Goldenen Fass.* He decides to sit down on the steps for a moment and rest. The blood in his mouth is obstructing his breathing. He opens his lips and lets it run down his chin and uniform.

'Hey, constable! You're bleeding!'

Nafzger opens his eyes a crack. A little man is standing in front of him – a labourer, to judge by his shabby attire and bad teeth. Leave me alone, thinks Nafzger. I'm tired.

'Constable! Constable!'

Nafzger pulls himself together. In order to get rid of the little man, he points in the direction of Sperrstrasse. 'Guns, those two, guns!'

The little man – Friedrich Zwahlen by name, 42 years old and a tiler by trade – turns just in time to see two young men disappearing into the mist. He hesitates for a moment, debating whether to minister to the policeman or take up the chase. Then the hunter in him triumphs over the Good Samaritan. He leaves Nafzger, runs off down Sperrstrasse and turns into the Riehenring, shouting and cursing and calling on everyone to join in the pursuit. Out of breath, he's afraid his quarry have given him the slip when two young men – well-dressed young men – round the corner of Amerbachstrasse and head in his direction. Zwahlen comes to a halt, breathing heavily, and blocks the pavement with outstretched arms.

'Wait, gentlemen!'

They stop short.

'What's eating you?' asks the taller of the two, smiling in a way that doesn't appeal to Zwahlen. He wonders how to respond to this impertinent question, but he's spared any further deliberation when the smiling youth takes a gun from his overcoat pocket.

Zwahlen is startled, but he doesn't know how lucky he is – the shorter of the two young men has fired off all his bullets in Hedwig Vetter's guesthouse.

'Go on!' cries the latter. The taller of the two pulls the trigger. There's a bang and Zwahlen measures his length on the pavement.

Five minutes later he's leaning breathlessly against a wall, surrounded by curious spectators. One of them produces a notebook and speaks to him. He's a reporter from the *National-Zeitung,* an ambitious young man with the darting eyes of a rodent and a smoker's yellow teeth. Stuck in his hatband is a card inscribed 'Press' in bold lettering. Zwahlen blurts out his story, which is reproduced verbatim in next day's edition:

'I had the presence of mind to turn my head aside and the bullet only grazed me from a range of six feet, but I pretended to be gravely wounded and sank to the ground. That was what saved my life: the criminals evidently thought they'd killed me, and they continued to make their getaway down Amerbachstrasse.'

However, Zwahlen does withhold one thing from the young reporter. When questioned by the police, he will recall that only the shorter robber ran off. The taller of the two stood looking down at him with his teeth bared and the gun muzzle pointing at his head. The wound to Zwahlen's right cheek was far from life-threatening, one could tell that at a glance. Even though it was oozing an impressive amount of blood, it looked more like a razor cut.

'The tall robber swore at me for being a snooper, a know-all and a goody-goody – I can't remember what else. He said I'd be wiser to look after my wife and children at home than chase after him and play the hero. When I said I was single and had no children, he yelled at me to go to a bar and drink a *café cognac* and pinch the barmaid's bottom. Then he turned on his heel and ran off after his accomplice.'

Zwahlen also tells the reporter from the *National-Zeitung*: 'As soon as I saw I was safe, I got up and resumed the chase with blood streaming down my face.

'I was yelling "Police!" at the top of my voice. The young men turned right into Hammerstrasse and appropriated two bicycles standing there. I ran after them as fast as I could, still shouting for help. I managed to draw the attention of passers-by to the criminals in this way, but when they saw my wound they just gawped at me like stuffed dummies.

'It wasn't until I reached Gottesackerstrasse that a policeman came to my aid. I quickly put him in the picture and he took up the chase, accompanied by numerous passers-by on foot and on bicycles.'

❧

Constable Alfred Nafzger is lying in the operating theatre in Basel's Bürgerspital, where bank officials Beutter and Kaufmann underwent surgery two weeks earlier. Standing beside him is Detective Corporal Maritz, who is anxious to obtain a description of the two wanted men. He is wearing sterile clothes, cap and mask, like a surgeon.

Maritz has no inkling that he himself is better placed than anyone to describe the pair, having only 14 hours earlier taken them to the police post and questioned them closely for at least 15 minutes.

The anaesthetist nurse is already busying herself with the chloroform mask and her colleagues are laying out instruments and infusing the patient. The senior surgeon pulls on his gloves and counsels haste.

'... I took a bullet in the back,' whispers Nafzger. 'I ran out onto the stairs at once and called for help. I think I heard some more shots, but I don't know what happened after that. I don't know what names were on the passports because Vollenweider didn't say them loud enough.' Then the anaesthetist turns on the tap. Alfred Nafzger, chairman of the Basel Police Federation and board member of the Basel Police Association, dies the next day without ever regaining consciousness.

15

Hedwig Vetter knows no peace that morning. There's a policeman lying dead in her best room, the stairs are covered in blood, and her boarders have been startled by gunfire. Many are hurriedly packing, others have already fled. The landlady hurries along the passages in search of outstanding rent, calling down curses on everything in general and the police in particular. At 7:43 am the doorbell rings.

'No vacancies!' shouts Hedwig Vetter. Then comes the sort of banging on the door that only policemen make. She fishes out her key and opens up. Policemen come swarming in. Snorting indignantly, the landlady jerks her chin at the stairs. The police photographer leads the way. He takes pictures of Police Corporal Vollenweider, whose lifeless body is still sprawled on the bed with his bowler hat stove in. He photographs the two open suitcases, the portable gramophone and the open ladies' umbrella lent to Velte only eight hours before, and his photographs make all these things look faded and forlorn, like belongings of the dead. Then it's the turn of his colleagues in forensics. They dust for fingerprints and search the beds, rummage in the suitcases and flick through the record album.

'Boss, look at this!' Someone holds up a photograph. It's one of the 14 pictures Waldemar and Kurt took in the Photomaton booth. The print goes off to the photographic laboratory with siren and flashing blue light escort, and an hour later every police station, frontier post and newsroom has a copy of it. Examination of the cartridge cases at Vollenweider's feet demonstrates that the same ammunition was used in the raid on the Wever Bank. Two grey-green raincoats and two pairs of motoring goggles are unearthed from beneath the mattresses.

Basel's entire police force is mobilised at once by a general alert. All off-duty uniformed policemen and detectives are summoned to headquarters in Lohndorf and from there fan out into the city. The frontier force college in nearby Liestal offers its services to the police. From Basel to Belfort, all crossing points into Alsace are placed on the alert, the Garde Mobile deploy on the French side, complete with steel helmets and carbines, mounted police patrol the German bank of the Rhine and the Reichswehr is called out. The frontier is hermetically sealed for 50 kilometres.

Completely unwitting, Dorly Schupp spends Saturday morning in the record department at Globus. It's quite busy. Waldemar and Kurt are probably on the train somewhere between Freiburg and Frankfurt. Kurt is bound to have chummed up with some girl and will be standing outside in the corridor with her while Waldemar sits in his window seat, staring out at the countryside.

At eleven o'clock Dorly hands over the till to the lunchtime shift and sets off for home. Now that the Christmas season is over and lunch breaks are longer, her mother cooks her a midday meal. In Marktplatz, she gets in at the very back of the tram. At the last moment, a newspaper boy jumps in up front beside the driver.

'Extra, extra! Policeman murdered in Sperrstrasse!'

Dorly cranes her neck. The passengers on either side of the aisle hold out coins and open their papers. The headline is unusually bold, but Dorly is too far away to decipher it. There's a fairly big picture in the middle of the front page. The newspaper boy sells papers right and left alternately. The bold lettering and the picture come nearer and nearer to Dorly. The picture displays two faces, two men. They look at Dorly in echelon, at least 20 of them in two rows. Bigger and bigger grow the black-and-white heads with their slicked-back hair and laughing mouths. A whole, laughing male voice choir is advancing on Dorly two abreast, and when the man in front of her spreads out the special edition she can also read the caption below the picture: 'The Murderers.'

Dorly leaves the tram and walks home. 'But I thought it must be a mistake, because I didn't believe them capable of such a crime. When I reached home I found a special edition there already, and it convinced me that they really must be the murderers. I told my mother I considered it my duty to give the police all the relevant information I possessed. My mother agreed, and I was just about to do what had to be done when Detective Corporal Maritz came to fetch me.'

Hans Maritz came across Dorly Schupp by chance. He had spent the morning going around the restaurants and hotels near the Central Station and showing waitresses the picture of Sandweg and Velte. 'At the *Markthalle* restaurant I discovered that the proprietor and waitresses were all well acquainted with the two murderers because they ate at the *Markthalle* almost daily. One of the waitresses went on to tell me that a Fraül-ein Schupp, a sales assistant at Globus, would be in a better position to give me some information – not that she had ever entered the restaurant – because she and the two Germans often met.'

By midday, therefore, Dorly Schupp is sitting at police headquarters and telling all she knows about Kurt Sandweg and Waldemar Velte. 'I never suspected that the pair and the bank robbers were one and the same. My mother was less surprised; she had always thought they were white slavers. It's true I became friendly with them, but I've no qualms about telling the police what I know about them. I'm not lying and have no secrets. I don't have to lie just because other people do.'

Dorly is allowed to leave once she has read through her statement and signed it. She goes out into the corridor, where radio and press reporters are waiting for news. The air is thick with tobacco smoke and a miasma of wet overcoats and half-digested sausage sandwiches and beer. None of the reporters takes any notice of Dorly Schupp because they're all intent on men today: district attorneys and detectives, villains and heroes, the wounded, the uninjured and the dead. A woman would interest them only if she gave off the sweet smell of fear and despair common to police widows and gangsters' molls.

Hour after uneventful hour goes by at headquarters. The miasma of sausage and beer steadily intensifies, the reporters grow impatient. Excited, blasé and bored in their habitual way, they trail after every policeman that appears.

'Any news?'

'Has that sighting in Kleinhüningen been confirmed?'

'What about the Reinach tip? No good either?'

'How many of you are on duty?'

'Four hundred? And still no trace of them?'

It has been like that since early this morning. Midday goes by and there's still no news. Time is running short. The radio needs something for the lunchtime news, the *National-Zeitung*'s editorial deadline for the evening edition expires at 2:00 pm, that of its competitor, *Basler Nachrichten,* half an hour later, and that of the *Arbeiter Zeitung* half an hour after that. Something has got to happen, but nothing does, so the reporters do what reporters the world over do in such emergencies: they interview each other. A local news reporter asks the correspondent of the *Petit Parisien* for an assessment of the situation and offers him one in return. Then they both hurry to the telephone to inform their editors of these new-found revelations. That fulfils their most pressing duty, and peace descends on the corridor. Many reporters, already half sozzled, lean against the wall and doze while others, not without pursing their lips derisively, read their competitors' effusions. Still others stand around in groups exchanging cigarettes and journalistic gossip. The atmosphere has become thoroughly agreeable – almost Mediterranean in its somnolence – when bells start ringing throughout the building. This means that the district attorney has sounded the alarm. Instantly, the news circulates like wildfire: 'The bank robbers have been sighted! Definitely! Eight kilometres outside town! At the Tschäpperli ruins near Dornach!'

16

Police boots go thundering along the corridors of the Lohnhof headquarters. Gun cabinets are wrenched open, carbines and steel helmets issued, police dogs collected from their kennels. Every available car and motorcycle is laden with policemen and sets off for the Basel hinterland.

Left behind are the journalists, who toss their sausage sandwiches and beer bottles into wastepaper baskets and try in vain to beg a ride. Not until the first private citizens volunteer to lend the police their cars for the manhunt does the district attorney permit journalists to come too, albeit at their own risk and expense.

The young reporter from the *National-Zeitung* wangles a place in the back of an Opel heading for the Jura with three detectives on board. 'We race up the Birsig Valley to Ettingen. From there our route takes us uphill through the forest, our car climbing the soft, slippery, muddy slope. Our three detectives have been instructed to follow the trail from the Tschäpperli ruins. We stop at the log cabin in the ravine and remove our safety catches. First we check the log cabin: all in order, doors and windows securely locked. We examine a wide area around the cabin for possible tracks while one of us remains on guard beside the car. We eagerly scan the thin covering of snow for footprints, zig-zagging back and forth through the trees as quietly as possible. All at once, on a steep, narrow path through the forest, we discover the fresh tracks of two people. We're all now convinced we're on the murderers' trail! We carefully follow these tracks, which at first lead steeply downwards. We come to a wide expanse of snow enclosed by a barbed-wire fence. There we temporarily lose the trail but soon pick it up again. It now leads to the right and up through the forest.'

❧

It is 5:00 pm and darkness is descending on the countryside. While the young reporter is hurrying through the forest after his three detectives, two young men with mud-smeared trousers enter the *Zum Bahnhof* restaurant in the small neighbouring town of Laufen. 'Evening all!' the taller of the two calls to the regulars in broad Swiss German. They sit down, and he orders rösti, sausages and a green salad for two. After they've eaten he calls for the bill. Then they disappear into the darkness. The waitress will shortly afterwards swear that the tall young man couldn't possibly be German because he spoke such perfect Baslerisch. She can't offer an opinion on his shorter companion because he remained silent the whole time.

❧

The *National-Zeitung* reporter is still stalking 'through the silent forest, never taking our eyes off the tracks. The blanket of snow becomes steadily thinner and more transparent – icy! – and it's getting dark. The tracks become increasingly difficult to detect and eventually disappear altogether into the darkness of night. What to do? Knowing roughly which way Zwingen lies, we decide to make for there. We stumble downhill over soft, muddy ground with clods of dirt clinging to our boots. Suddenly, human voices. We steal carefully up the slope, guns at the ready. A gipsy encampment! To loud curses from its nomadic inhabitants, it is carefully searched. Further on we come to a lonely farm, the "Rote Grube". A motorcycle patrol has raced through there shortly before us and warned the farming folk about the murderers. Farmhands show us the way down the valley. Just before Zwingen we encounter a motorised police patrol. It gives us a lift to the town, where we also find our own car, which has arrived in the meantime. Shortly before seven we sit down in a small inn and have a drink. All at once a mud-spattered policeman bursts in. Extremely agitated, he blurts out: "They've gone and shot another two policemen!"'

A few minutes earlier … A motorcycle-sidecar combination driven by 56-year-old Detective Constable Walter Gohl is nearing the little town of Laufen. Ensconced in the sidecar is Detective Corporal Hans Maritz, who has, in the past 24 hours, questioned Kurt Sandweg, Waldemar Velte, the mortally wounded Constable Alfred Nafzger, and Dorly Schupp in quick succession. Five hundred metres short of Laufen the motorcycle passes a quarry in the darkness on the right. Hans Maritz, who is due to celebrate 25 years in the force in three months' time, believes he has spotted something suspicious in the quarry. He signs to Gohl to go back. The motorcycle turns round and slowly approaches the quarry. Then five shots ring out in the darkness. The first two hit Detective Corporal Maritz in the head and kill him instantly. The third shot shatters Gohl's lower jaw, the fourth and fifth pierce his chest.

17

People flock together everywhere when the latest atrocity becomes known. Family men take their carbines from the wardrobe and load them with deliberation while their wives secure the shutters. Dozens of men armed with scythes, pitchforks, pistols and rifles congregate outside every police station. 'It has now been decided,' wrote the reporter from the *National-Zeitung*, 'to hunt those murderers down without mercy. "Dead or alive!" – that was the watchword.'

The little town of Laufen is swarming with policemen. Early that evening they are reinforced by the arrival of detachments from the neighbouring cantons of Bern, Baselland and Solothurn. Every hotel, guesthouse and restaurant is reserved for the police. The streets resound with shouted orders and the barking of dogs. Gun barrels and bayonets glint in the light of the street lamps.

By 10:00 that night, the area around Laufen is sealed within a radius of 25 kilometres. All the bridges are closely watched, all the roads closed. For safety's sake, police officers are instructed to stand guard in the lee of hedges and bushes, not in the middle of the road.

In view of this sabre-rattling invasion, the local inhabitants no longer leave their homes. Those who do venture out into the street for any reason will be confronted at every turn by cocked pistols and nervous figures in uniform. Unhappiest of all are the children, who are not allowed out; they all want to play cops and robbers on such an exciting evening, and it's no fun doing that in the living room. Bigger boys refuse to be dictated to, however, and deliberately sally forth into the dangerous darkness.

Twenty-one-year-old Franz Zellweger leaves his uncle's house and crosses the gravelled forecourt to the garage. He gets out the motorbike Uncle Hans gave him for graduating from non-commissioned officers' school, a black, two-cylinder, 750 cc BMW R16. Franz has long legs, broad shoulders and white teeth, and he's the most promising sprig of a prosperous family of Laufen industrialists. All this appeals to girls, and Franz knows it. His elderly Uncle Hans owns a cork-processing factory with widespread subsidiaries, and he's childless. Now that Franz has completed his military service, the old man has taken him on at his head office in Laufen, where he can groom him to take over the business. Franz Zellweger kicks the BMW into life and roars off into the night to capture the bank robbers. If the police aren't up to it, he'll have to lend them a hand.

'That Zellweger boy was a coxcomb,' declared my grandfather 50 years later. He spoke with unwonted vehemence after I'd repeated my question three times. We were picking the Boskoop apples and his feet were three rungs up the ladder from my hands, so he couldn't escape. 'A coxcomb, nothing more. I knew him quite well. After all, we were both athletes, singers, Free Democrats, and …' – he harrumphed – '… of good family. I'm not saying he deserved what happened to him, but he was a coxcomb. A sweet-talker with lots of Brilliantine in his hair. Thought he was God's gift to girls, but girls don't care for types like him, take it from me.'

❧

Franz Zellweger's best friend is waiting for him at the town gate. Franz stops to let him get on. Nobody knows the friend's name or identity to this day, because for one thing, boys like Franz Zellweger usually pick insignificant individuals to be their best friends, and for another, the press and police suppressed his name for reasons of personal privacy and simply referred to him as 'Franz Zellweger's best friend'.

So that night the two friends ride the BMW out of town and come to a roadblock, where they're made to identify themselves. Franz Zellweger dismounts and engages the policeman on duty in conversation. Like any sprig of a wealthy family, he feels convinced that all public servants live off his taxes and are, strictly speaking, his personal assistants. After a few friendly remarks, he jovially slaps the policeman – who is old enough to be his father – on the back, utters some words of encouragement, and returns to his motorbike. At this moment a blue light comes flashing past. It's the ambulance taking Walter Gohl, the wounded detective, to the Bürgerspital in Basel. Hans Maritz's corpse is still lying in the quarry.

Franz Zellweger and his best friend set off again and drive past the quarry. A hundred metres further on, Franz spots a car half hidden in the bushes. He pulls up and directs his headlight at it. Seated in the car are two men in civilian clothes. Franz kills the engine, tells his friend to get off, heaves the machine on to its stand, and dismounts too.

'Hands up!' Police Constable Stehlin calls from inside the

car. Franz Zellweger and his best friend hesitate for a moment, whereupon Stehlin, who is under strict orders from his squad commander to use lethal force if necessary, pulls the trigger. 'Oh, goddammit!' Zellweger exclaims in an unmistakably Baselland accent, and he falls to the ground with a bullet through the lung.

When Police Constable Stehlin discovers his mistake, he runs off into the darkness and doesn't come back. Two hours later, two colleagues who go in search of him find him sitting on his heels in a dip at the foot of a pine tree, rocking back and forth and weeping.

The *National-Zeitung,* writing of Franz Zellweger's funeral four days later: 'It was unforgettably moving to see the unfortunate policeman who had fired the fatal shot, and had appeared at the graveside in spite of his nervous breakdown, dissolve into tears and pour out his unspeakable sorrow in the arms of the deceased's family members.'

❧

My grandfather knew a lot about motorbikes as well as cars. 'The BMW R16 was a luxury bike, you know. Typical of Zellweger. Cost 2040 marks, even during the Depression. BMW produced and sold only 1106 of them in five years. I'd have liked one too, of course. Two-cylinder boxer engine with overhead valves, 25 horsepower, maximum speed 140 kilometres per hour. The Germans went to war with its successor, the R12, incidentally. BMW delivered 16,500 of them to the Wehrmacht alone. Most of them got stuck in the Russian mud. A good thing for the Russians and the rest of us, pity about the motorbikes.'

❧

After the fatal shots in the quarry, operational headquarters confines all mobile patrols to their billets for safety's sake. The manhunt is postponed until daybreak, though the roadblocks remain in place. The officers return to their hotel rooms, the other ranks lie down to sleep in gymnasiums and stables, the dogs curl up and bury their noses in their fur.

18

8:00 am on Sunday, 21 January 1934. Dawn is breaking, Laufen waking up. Hobnailed police boots clatter on cobblestones, engines warm up, enamel mugs of coffee disseminate their aroma. In a field outside town is a biplane, its propeller blasting the hoarfrost off the grass stems and whirling it into the air. Standing beside the machine are two police officers and the pilot. The policemen salute, military fashion; the airman casually taps his leather helmet, then climbs into the cockpit and opens the throttle. The biplane lumbers across the turf and takes off, skimming low over the treetops of a small pine wood. The pine trees sway, and dislodged snow falls to the forest floor on which Kurt Sandweg and Waldemar Velte are sleeping. They are lying back to belly on Waldemar's overcoat with Kurt's overcoat serving as a blanket. The snow falling from the treetops wakes Waldemar. He extricates himself from his friend's embrace, crawls out from between the coats, and takes a small, black, oilskin-covered notebook from his pocket.

'The last day of my life: Sunday, 21.1.1934. At the moment it's 8:10 am. The two of us reached Laufen after superhuman exertions, half-starved and dead beat. (Last night.) Had something to eat there and were promptly recognised, much to the detriment of two policemen. We spent the night in the woods in freezing temperatures, having seen that escape was impossible. So we took death for granted. That was fine with us because it meant supreme happiness. We'll at last be free of all this wretchedness and misery. The whole thing was bound to end like this.

'We two are endowed by nature with a keen sense of justice and have tried from an early age to think logically and act consistently instead of forever stifling our sensitive consciences over the course of the years, as dear old human society must in order to be able to exist.

'We intensified our sense of justice and search for objective truth still further, and such an attitude, which is the only correct one, inevitably brought us into conflict with "dear old human society". We knew exactly where we were headed.

'There isn't a jot of difference between the course of our actions hitherto and their consequences, so we have no regrets and are not disappointed. On the contrary, we're pleased we had the strength to fight for the one true *raison d'être.* We won't have to return to this hell known as the "world". We shall be free of it.

'People will have to suffer a hundredfold for having raised their hands against us. Those who preserve goodness and ideals kill God. So have you ever considered, you leading politicians, lawyers, district attorneys, judges and police commissioners, that you'll sometime have to suffer terribly for your profession, and that you'll be privileged to return to this "beautiful" earth? If you had even a scrap of natural understanding, you'd weep for yourselves. You too will someday have to tread our path! That's as certain as a Gospel. Lots of luck, you criminals – a mild term for people of your stamp. The only pity is you've never crossed our path, you cunning devils. We would like to have had a bit of a talk about politics, you "sound fellows"! But you'll get your come-uppance! That's a law of nature. It makes you think and come to the right conclusion!

'We've got it behind us. If there were fewer people in the world, life might still be possible; but wherever the miserable creatures known as men have their finger in the pie, everything is botched and wrecked. It isn't enough that they are their own worst enemies – no, not even the loveliest parts of the natural world are sacrosanct from their atrocities. Yet they convict themselves by their own behaviour. Their life and their fate are governed by it. They will all have to come back many times before they reach the right conclusion.

'If you make your own bed, you must lie in it.

'Instead of using their intelligence to redeem themselves, they have built up a world of illusion, of folly, and it will one day prove their undoing. There have been too few people prepared to lay down their lives for what they perceive, which is why they are now all so bad and further removed than ever from life's true purpose. But they must go their own way; and if they were sensible, they would ensure that it was as short as possible. But insanity rules the world. On the one hand, people build palatial art galleries; on the other, countless thousands starve to death and degenerate in the direst poverty. This is where the unnaturalness of the masses takes its revenge, for if they had remained on the right road, the "national leaders" – or rather, seducers – would never have dared to commit such heinous sins against nature. They would have been summarily killed. On the contrary, the masses are crazy enough to persecute and arrest those who oppose such abominations and thereby indirectly champion the common good – and all for "dear old justice" in the shape of a reward.

'You stupid policemen, hasn't it dawned on you what crime you've committed against yourselves?? Don't you realise that all you're doing in practice is ensuring that you meet a ridiculous end? You would do better to hang yourselves rather than be the tools of "creatures" who daily betray and lie to you and your kind. But you are also not exempt from treading the lamentable path your "masters" must travel.'

Then Waldemar Velte begins a new page:

'Please, in the event of my death, send this to my parents in Wuppertal.

'Dear ones! My hour will soon have struck. I'm glad. I'm sick of people, and because people are the world's principal feature, it has lost its appeal for me. How will you judge me? I already know. You've never understood me. To your misfortune, for now something so terrible – by your standards – has happened, you couldn't really go on living. It isn't my fault. I can't, out of consideration for you, do wrong. Bring up Hilde and Lothar as I would, so that their sufferings are short, or their life, too, will be one long round of sorrow, humiliation and vileness. They, like you, will one day have to go the same way as me. So bear that in mind. We won't see each other again down here, but I'll always be with you. Farewell!!! The "tools" are already quite close and are looking for us. They want to earn their reward, the righteous creatures, but it won't be so easy. Farewell. Give my love to all our relations and tell them not to rush to judgement.'

Kurt Sandweg wakes up while Waldemar Velte is writing. He asks him to pass the notebook and the pencil.

'Dear Mother, we shall soon be in a better place. Don't worry, we're happy to go, you know that. We shall see each other again there! Let people talk; they would have done better to help, because we didn't like doing what we did. Many thanks for everything. I can't repay you, alas. Yours, Kurt.'

Then Waldemar Velte writes to Kurt Sandweg's mother.

'Dear Frau Sandweg, our last hour has come. We seem to have fulfilled our *raison d'être.* Thus do idealists end! Or ought we to sing from the same hymn sheet as international crooks? Honesty prevents us from doing so. We die gladly. This hell holds no charms for us. Many thanks for all your kindness to me. I'd have liked to repay it, but I wasn't granted that opportunity. So Kurt and I take our leave of you in everlasting remembrance. We shall all see each other again on a better star. Let's hope there aren't so many miserable people there. Goodbye!'

While Kurt and Waldemar are waiting for uniformed figures to rush them, a surprising thing takes place on the edge of the forest: the soldiers leave their firing positions, the policemen remove their nailed planks from the roads, the frontier guards put their dogs on a short leash, and they all board their cars, motorcycles and lorries and drive off. The blockade is lifted. Operational headquarters has come to the conclusion that the bank robbers must have managed to slip through the police cordon under cover of darkness.

19

The biplane circles over the Basel hinterland for hour after hour. The pilot doggedly keeps watch, occasionally committing minor frontier violations on the French or German side of the border. He continues to circle, but there's no sign of Sandweg and Velte.

ℰ𝒮

Down on the ground, Marie Stifter and Ernst Walder were sitting on the bench outside the post office, closely watching the aeroplane. Marie regarded it as an enemy because it was after her friend and Ernst regarded it as a friend because it was after his enemy, but they would never have admitted this to each other.

After the kiss that sealed their betrothal two weeks earlier, Ernst had resumed his ritual lunchtime visits. It was now Marie, not her mother the postmistress, who sat waiting on the garden bench beside Hasso, the Appenzeller Mountain Dog. When Ernst drew near she waved to him and gave him a dutiful smile; he waved as he approached and endeavoured to look friendly. Conversation dragged as usual, and they often sat beside each other in silence for minutes on end.

'You'd better go,' she said. 'It's time for your football practice.'

Ernst shook his head. 'Training's been cancelled.'

'Oh.'

'Until further notice.'

'Pity.'

'I can make up for it later.'

'Yes.'

'Before Mass I spoke to one of the two policemen guarding Dorfstrasse. They've no idea what the score is – don't know which way to turn.'

'Really?'

'They get reports from all over the place, but they're all false alarms. The robbers are said to have turned up thirty kilometres south of here, but also ten kilometres to the north and even over in France.'

Marie said nothing, but little crow's feet of amusement formed at the corners of her eyes and her lower lip jutted scornfully. Ernst saw this and it annoyed him. His fiancée evidently considered it good news that the murderers were making fools of the police. The aeroplane continued to circle in the sky.

'Then there are people who deliberately put the police on the wrong track. Just imagine, last night they arrested two students in Laufen. They'd come from Bern specially, just to murmur textbook German in bars and peer around as if they were on the run.'

'You don't say.'

'Yes, and two locals stole a factory worker's purse. Two 18-year-olds. They called out "Your money or your life!" in a bad German accent.'

'No.'

'Yes. Then they opened his purse and laughed because there

was so little in it. And then they chucked the purse at his feet and disappeared into the darkness.'

'And is that why your football practice has been cancelled?'

'What do you mean?'

'Because of those youngsters?'

'No, not because of them.' Ernst clenched his teeth so hard, his jaw clicked for the first time in his life. 'It's because the police are advising people to stay indoors.'

'Well, in that case ...'

'It's dangerous. They shot a civilian by mistake last night. Franz Zellweger from Laufen.'

Grandmother should, of course, have greeted this news with an exclamation, a word, or just a noise of some kind. Instead, she preserved an eloquent female silence lasting three or four seconds. Then, in the most innocent voice imaginable, she said: 'So does that mean you'll be staying indoors till the danger's over?'

Grandfather's only possible response to that was a contemptuous snort. 'We'll see. Maybe I'll go and do some training after all. I'll ask Benno if he'll come too. He's our centre forward.'

❧

The biplane is still airborne an hour later. It will soon run out of fuel. Then it will have to land the way it did two hours ago. But look! Two men are running across open ground down there! They're undoubtedly young and they're going flat out, judging by the way they're running across that field, and one of them looks a bit taller than the other! The pilot banks away and flies back to Laufen. He takes his note pad from a side pocket and writes: 'The two fugitives definitely sighted in the

Laufen-Wahlen-Fehren area!' He inserts the slip of paper in a leather pouch and tosses it out over the landing field. Then he circles above the little town, waits for the police to board their lorries, and flies on ahead with the convoy following. He can already see the suspects up ahead, one tall, the other shorter. They have turned round and are actually running towards the police lorries. The latter screech to a halt, the policemen jump out and hurl themselves into ditches. There's a clatter of rifle bolts. The two suspects slow down, come to a halt, and cast curious glances at the hundred gun barrels into whose field of fire they have strayed. White vapour issues from the runners' mouths, white vapour from those of the policemen.

'Well?' asks the shorter of the two. 'Caught them yet?'

'No!' calls an anonymous constable.

'Lots of luck!' calls the taller of the two, and they set off again. The policemen stare after them. Both runners are wearing black Nabholz tracksuits with diagonal white stripes across the chest, and the taller one is audibly clicking his jaw.

❧

The young reporter from the *National-Zeitung* is sitting over his notepad in the *Rössli* restaurant in Laufen, taking stock. 'The police dogs have been a total failure, because not even the keenest nose can pick up a scent on frozen ground. Another two hours have gone by, and there's still nothing new to report. We're all smoking like chimneys to prevent ourselves from falling asleep. It almost looks as if this great day is going to end in an equally great disappointment because, to sum up the results of this day of grand strategy, it must sadly be stated that there's no definite trace of the murderers. The encircled area looks small on the map but is really vast in extent. The famous manhunt in the woods that was yesterday expected to achieve such decisive results has been repeatedly postponed. It almost seems as if those in command are renouncing the implementation of this plan – because it's hopeless. The police are going to wait another two hours, but then the order to go home will be issued.'

20

Ten pm. Sunday night. Dorly Schupp has spent the entire weekend holed up at home. Her mother's implacable air of martyrdom has been hard to endure: the pursed lips, the prominent, concentric veins around the eyes, the silence, the ticking of the wall clock; but even harder to bear would have been the neighbours' inquisitive glances, her workmates' sympathetic chatter and the whispers of strangers in the streets. It's time for bed. Dorly is combing her hair at the washstand in her nightgown when the bell in the passage rings. 'I knew at once that it could only be Sandweg and Velte. I sent my mother to our neighbours on the second floor to alert the police while I went upstairs to the Herzog family's phone on the third. So it was my definite intention to alert the police. I sent my mother on ahead so as to waste no time.'

Transcript of a telephone conversation between Viktoria Schupp and Kurt Sandweg, monitored by Detective Corporal M Werner at 10:13 pm on Sunday, 21 January 1934:

'Hello, Viktoria Schupp here.'
'Ah, so it's you, Fraülein Dorly.'
'Kurt! But this is terrible, this is awful!'
'No, Dorly, don't get upset. It isn't awful, it's nothing at all.'

'You idiot! Where are you both?'

'Quite near. In the big park behind the station.'

'What? Here in Basel?'

'Yes.'

'Are you mad? Which park?'

'The one behind the station.'

'The one with the ice rink?'

'Yes, that's it.'

'Is Waldemar there too?'

'Not with me, actually, but close by. Here in the park. Listen, Fraülein Dorly, could you please bring us something to eat?'

'What?'

'We're terribly hungry.'

'But … all right. Where shall I meet you?'

'In Höhenweg, by the Astronomical Institute. I'll whistle.'

'What should I bring?'

'Anything, it doesn't matter what. Some bread.'

'All right.'

'Fraülein Dorly?'

'Yes?'

'How long will you be?'

'Well, quite a while, I was just going to bed. I'll have to get dressed first, and it'll take me a while to get there. You'll just have to wait till I come.'

'I understand. I'm sorry we're putting you to this trouble. They're after us, as you probably know.'

'Yes. Then I'll go and get ready now.'

'Yes. Thanks a lot, Fraülein Dorly.'

'See you soon.'

'See you soon.'

'I just had time to get dressed before a police car came to collect me and pulled up outside the building. After I'd been asked several times whether I would go to meet the two of them in the park, I said yes – not because I wanted to see them again, but because I reckoned it would assist the police in capturing the murderers. I got out of the car in Margarethenstrasse, made my way to Batterieweg via Gundeldingerstrasse, and when I reached the south entrance to the park, which is in Höhenweg, I heard a low whistle and the words: "Fraülein Dorly, come into the park." The gate was open. I climbed the wooden steps leading from the gate into the park and saw the two of them standing side by side on the path immediately below the steps. They were both holding pistols and staring at me. They were in a very dishevelled state and had swapped overcoats. Sandweg was wearing the dark one and Velte the grey, speckled one. Velte just stared at me in total silence. I then handed him the little package I'd brought, which contained a pound loaf. He took it without a word. It's true that I'd wrapped the bread in the special edition of the *National-Zeitung* that gave a detailed report of the murder in Sperrstrasse, wanting to make it clear to them what they'd done. I drew their attention to the newspaper, but they took no notice of it.

'I can't say whether they'd fallen out with each other. Velte was looking gloomy. Sandweg's manner was friendly, in fact I even saw him smile. The general atmosphere was grim and they both seemed mentally drained. I gained the impression, especially from Velte, that they thought they were done for. In retrospect, I'm sure that by that stage they'd abandoned all hope of leaving Margarethen Park alive.

'I addressed them in a low voice, saying: "Really, really, what have you done!" To which Velte replied: "Take it easy, Fraülein

Dorly. Have you seen any policemen?" "No," I replied, "I came up the back way and didn't see anyone." Sandweg patted me on the shoulder with the hand holding the gun and said: "It's kind of you to have come."

'I asked Sandweg why they'd swapped overcoats. He said Velte had felt so cold in his sodden overcoat, he'd given him his own because it was a bit drier. He'd been looking in the direction of Binningen while speaking, in other words, at the edge of the park. Suddenly he gave a start and called out, quite loudly: "Hey, police!" He grabbed Velte's arm and they ran off down the path into the park. The fact that they held each other by the arm while running away suggested that the peace that had reigned between them previously still prevailed.

'I stayed where I was until they were out of sight and I couldn't hear their footsteps any longer. Then I climbed back up the wooden steps and went out into Höhenweg, where I was met by several policemen. Being exhausted, I lay down for some time on the grass behind the police cordon.'

❧

Dorly lies down on last summer's brittle grass and looks up at the night sky, which the west wind has rent open. The edges of the clouds are white with moonlight, and a few stars are twinkling in the black voids between them. Stationed beneath each tree on the outskirts of the park is a uniformed policeman, each wearing a steel helmet and holding a rifle, and each staring into the gloomy park and waiting for dawn. From time to time, men in plain clothes flit from tree to tree and policeman to policeman, whispering instructions. One of them notices Dorly and comes over to her. It's Senior District Attorney Stephan

Hungerbühler. He points out that the ground is frozen and she'll catch her death, takes her by the hand and tries to haul her to her feet, but Dorly snatches her hand away and asks him to let her lie there a little longer. The district attorney goes off and returns with two woollen blankets. One he spreads out beside her, the other he leaves nearby.

'So as not to seem ungrateful, I lay down on one of the blankets and spread the other over myself. A few moments later, two shots rang out in quick succession; in fact I initially thought it was only one. The shots came perhaps ten or fifteen minutes after my conversation with Sandweg and Velte. They shocked me to the core, not only because of my platonic love for Velte and my friendship with Sandweg, but because of the thought that bullets had been fired at human beings in my presence.'

Dorly pulls the blanket over her head, turns on her side and draws her knees up. Passing policemen regard the bundle of humanity beneath the blanket with raised eyebrows, slow down for a moment, and then walk on quickly. In the city, the first church clock strikes midnight, then all the others join in. When silence returns, two more shots ring out. This time there are definitely two. One shot, silence, then another.

'I was completely done in after those last shots. I got to my feet, folded up the blankets, took them over to the nearest policeman, and asked to be driven home. My request was granted at once. Back in my room, I flopped down on the bed without removing my shoes and coat and fell into a deep sleep of exhaustion from which I didn't awaken until lunchtime the next day. For the first few minutes I scarcely remembered the events of the previous night, and when they finally came back to me the whole thing seemed utterly unreal.'

❦

'Hey, police!' Kurt had cried, and then the pair had fled into the depths of the park, Kurt with pistol in hand, Waldemar hugging the loaf firmly to his chest. Out of sight, they had slumped down on a park bench and Waldemar had taken out his oilcloth-covered notebook once more.

'Dear Dorly, forgive me for doing this to you. We meant to do the right thing. The world is too bad a place for us. Bury me at the Hörnli. Kurt sends his love too. We shall see each other again. We were as good as the others say we're bad. A last goodbye, farewell! The two of us belong together. You're my life's greatest happiness. My only sunshine.'

While Dorly Schupp is spreading out a woollen blanket only a stone's throw away, Sandweg and Velte get up off the bench. Dorly lies down on the blanket, Kurt and Waldemar take their pistols from their overcoat pockets and hold them to each other's right temple. Dorly drapes the second blanket over herself. Waldemar and Kurt count to three and pull the trigger. Yet again, Waldemar Velte is a trifle more determined to stop at nothing.

'It's exactly five minutes past midnight. My shot to the head hasn't worked. I've given Kurt another and one in the heart.'

As Dorly Schupp is folding up the blankets and getting into the police car, Waldemar resumes his seat on the bench with Kurt's body twitching at his feet and the loaf wrapped in newspaper on the bench beside him. Without touching the loaf, he sits there like that for one, two, three, four, five, six hours. Shortly before seven o'clock, the sky between the leafless trees starts to pale. Dorly is fast asleep when Waldemar Velte rises to his feet under the gaze of 800 policemen, unbuttons his overcoat, reaches into the pocket, draws the gun, puts the muzzle to his chest, and pulls the trigger.

☙

Otto Beck, a police constable from the St Clare precinct: 'Together with some other policemen, I dashed over to the bench the two murderers were lying in front of. I saw that Velte's hands were still twitching, and that his pistol was lying on the ground to the right of his body.'

21

Moments later, people came storming into Margarethen Park from all directions. Foremost among them, once again, was the reporter from the *National-Zeitung.* 'News of the murderers' deaths spread through the city like wildfire, and thousands of people came hurrying up into Margarethen Park. The police permitted no one to approach the dead bodies until the police photographer had reached the spot with his camera and succeeded in photographing the corpses from every angle. Meantime, the hearse had driven up to the street above Margarethen Park. Two metal coffins were carried over to the bodies. First, detectives searched the murderers' pockets. The two guns were lying on the ground beside them. One contained a magazine still holding six rounds, the other seven! The murderers also had two full magazines in their pockets, each containing eight rounds. When the bodies had been placed in the coffins, they were carried to the hearse and driven away.'

The vehicle drove to Basel University's Anatomical Institute. There a man in a white gown sawed open Kurt Sandweg's skull and found two bullets in his brain. One had entered through the left temple, the other through the right. The third bullet had ruptured Sandweg's carotid artery. According to the forensic pathologist's report, any one of those wounds would have been fatal. Waldemar Velte's head displayed a superficial bullet wound two centimetres long. It had not injured the brain, but the shot in the heart must have killed him instantly.

The man in the white gown replaced the crania, sewed up the scalps, and carefully combed the hair over the stitches. He washed off the dried blood and pressed the rigid facial muscles back into place. Then he liberally smeared Sandweg's and Velte's faces with Vaseline, mixed up a good kilogramme of plaster of Paris, spread it over the faces, and waited for it to harden. Having smeared the hollow moulds with Vaseline in their turn, he filled them with plaster. Then he wheeled the corpses over to the cold store on their mobile examination tables, washed his hands, removed his gown, and went home for lunch.

❧

Dorly Schupp: 'We often passed Margarethen Park on our walks but never walked right across the park itself. On one occasion we entered it by the same gate I used that tragic night and sat down on the bench where the bodies of the two men were subsequently found. We remained there for only about 20 minutes because of the cold. I can't recall exactly when this was.'

❧

The plaster had hardened by half past one. The man in the white gown removed the death masks from the hollow moulds, applied a primer, and painted the faces true to life, paying special attention to the bullet holes, dental defects and skin blemishes. That done, he refilled the hollow moulds with plaster because he had been instructed to produce three pairs of death masks: one for the Basel police and one each for the German and French authorities.

&

The *National-Zeitung*: 'Another very interesting detail may be reported in this connection. It was incredibly fortuitous that the murderers telephoned that shop assistant and thereby sealed their fate! Situated on the ice rink construction site are TWO BUILDERS' HUTS. The robbers broke into one of those huts and found, not bread, but – a TELEPHONE. Probably half starved by then and at the end of their tether, they were so desperate that they had no recourse but to make that fateful telephone call. What if they had happened to break into the other hut? They would probably have jumped for joy, because that one contained AN ABUNDANCE OF FOOD: bread, cheese, sausage, ham – plus wine and beer! We can all picture the end of the story for ourselves.'

22

On Monday the leader writers took stock of the drama, all in their own different ways. Under the headline 'Göringian Brownshirt Bandits Murder in Basel. Basel Police Incompetent Versus Criminals but Tough on Workers', the editor of the communist daily *Vorwärts* wrote: 'Nothing like these frightful murders can hitherto be found in the annals of local crime. What sort of mentality is it that gave rise to this series of diabolically cold-blooded crimes? It is morphine-addict Göring's "open fire" decree that gives revolvers free rein. Where mass murderers exist, shouldn't there be little brutes as well? It would be surprising if there weren't!'

The *Katholisches Volksblatt* took a different view: 'Sandweg and Velte's ruthlessness and recklessness are characteristic of the public danger represented by abominable individuals in the devil's guise. Inhumanity of this order is cogent evidence of brutalisation in regard to higher values such as life and property, ethics and morals, particularly in the young. Lack of faith and godlessness are much to blame for this decadence.'

To this, the social democratic *Arbeiter-Zeitung* rejoined: 'I ask you: Is respect for human life really so sacred to all who are crying out for expiation? Don't our worthy employers find it axiomatic that their male and female workers should daily risk their lives for entrepreneurial gain and their own vital necessities? Who gets up in arms when one of them has to depart this life?

'Where is the respect for human life when a shipping company, for love of profit and in the hope of pocketing a big insurance pay-out, heavily insures an old tub and, regardless of those on board, sends it to sea with a worthless cargo on the assumption that it will sink? Is their indignation at the crime genuine, who abhor murder in this case but promote and are even complicit in another version of it? We still remember how, during the war, reports from the front were read by a sensation-seeking class of people who took note of 10,000 dead and 30,000 wounded between soup and main course. Where is the indignation at all these murders today, when the fascist press instigates murder from political calculation?'

The *Basler-Nachrichten,* 'Basel's paper for the thinking reader', expressed surprise at the fact that Sandweg and Velte 'had rebelled against the existing social order even though they had absolutely no reason to do so, their fathers being prosperous and extremely popular businessmen. In other respects, the drama indicates that a substantial percentage of crimes are being committed by individuals from abroad. If this is really so, it sheds more light on the refugee question. This country's security must not be compromised by the right of asylum. All else apart, there is a danger that it will promote a psychotic antipathy to foreigners.'

German newspapers tended to find the affair embarrassing. On 1 February the *Stuttgarter Neues Tagblatt* wrote: '... we report these latest results of police investigations, albeit with a certain inner reluctance, because it almost appears to us as if unremitting preoccupation with the two criminals and the motives for their crimes is ascribing too much importance to the persons concerned. The same applies to their jottings, which should probably be regarded as products of mentally immature and morally depraved persons. The case, whose brutality is plain enough, ought not to be complicated by a surfeit of psychology.'

The *Schwäbischer Merkur* stated: 'If they could have been captured on German territory, they would in any case have perished under the executioner's axe. Not so in Switzerland, however, where the death penalty does not exist.'

In the youth supplement of the *Basler Arbeiter-Zeitung,* a girl wrote: 'So much has been written, so much shouted about Velte and Sandweg on all sides and in the same vein: Murderers, brutes, Brownshirt bandits! One has become utterly saddened, utterly tired, because people are so blinkered. Is that really all there is to be said about the pair? Didn't we feel anything else about their fate?

'We grew up in the same era as them and have had to experience the world as they did, a world that gives young people no space, no scope for making the most of their talents, and has only one thing to offer: unemployment.

'Living in this world are young people, gifted and full of energy, filled with a desire to make use of their abilities and have a place in life. Society cannot employ them. Isn't it understandable that they should turn their energy against that society?

'Velte and Sandweg possessed courage and enterprise; they wanted life to demand a great effort from them. Unemployment and hopelessness aroused their hatred of their whole environment. They fought that enemy with all their might. Having been offered no task in life, they created a task in which they could employ their energies. Is it so incomprehensible that the lives of others mean less when one is recklessly gambling with one's own?

'True, they conducted their campaign against society in an altogether wrong and irrational manner, but can a world devoid of reason expect people to act rationally?

'People of lesser stature gradually become inured to the lunacy of this age and drift along with it, but it can drive people of greater stature mad. The death of the pair has demonstrated that they were persons of high calibre. Their faith in the girl displayed their inherent goodness and nobility.

'Comrades! Let us remember Waldemar Velte and Kurt Sandweg with affection and understanding. Let us, with renewed determination, combat a society that drives people of merit to tread an irrational path!'

Responding to this the next day, an older comrade wrote: 'I also regard the pair as victims of society, and of specifically German social conditions – victims of that frightful military upbringing which turns war into a cult and makes it everyone's task to eliminate as many of his fellow creatures as possible. Had Sandweg and Velte shot or "disposed of" some Social Democrats in Germany, rather than bank employees in Stuttgart or Basel, they would now be bathed in the aura of the Third Reich and enjoying the favour of Hitler, Göring and Co. Because they did not do so, not even their death renders them "persons of high calibre", imbued with "inherent goodness and nobility", whom young socialists can "remember with affection and understanding".

'I protest against such a purportedly socio-critical assessment, which is really a sentimental, kitschy glorification that seems to me to stem from a Karl May psychosis. The deaths of Sandweg and Velte and all their victims are to be deplored, but the two men are no heroes of socialist youth.

'By saying this I may be relegated to the "people of lesser stature", but since, as a socialist, I cannot lead the same life as Velte and Sandweg, nor will my death prove that I am to be numbered among the "persons of high calibre".'

23

My grandfather brought no roses with him when he turned up at the post office the following Tuesday. Instead, he came bearing a rolled-up morning edition of the *National-Zeitung* and slapped his thigh with it at every step. He sat down on the bench beside my grandmother, smoothed the paper out on his lap, rolled it up again and smoothed it out once more.

'No training today?' asked my grandmother.

'Read the paper yet?' he rejoined.

'I never read the paper.'

'Those two murderers were buried yesterday.'

'Really?'

'In Basel. In anonymous coroner's graves.'

'Mhm?'

'Suicides aren't entitled to a Christian burial.'

'Mhm.'

'Shall I read it to you?'

Marie didn't reply. She stared straight ahead at the road, which was deserted at this peaceful, lunchtime hour. Ernst opened the paper and read aloud: '"The Basel district attorney's office enquired via the police radio in Wuppertal what was to be done with Sandweg and Velte's bodies. Both families dispensed with repatriation. Although Waldemar Velte's father initially telegraphed his intention of attending the burial in

Basel, he later, on being questioned again, said that he would refrain from making the journey for financial reasons. The district attorney then rescinded the confiscation of the corpses." Shall I read on?'

'If you like.'

'I don't have to.'

'Why do you want to read it to me?'

'Just because.'

'You think it ought to interest me?'

'No,' said Ernst.

'All right, where are they buried? At the Hörnli?'

'Why at the Hörnli?'

'Only asking. Where, then?'

'Just a moment.' He opened the paper. 'It says here, at the Wolf Cemetery. I've no idea where that is.'

'I do, though. Between the goods station and the football stadium.'

'Aha.' Ernst gave Marie a suspicious sidelong glance. 'How do you know that?'

'An aunt of mine is buried there.'

'Really?'

'Aunt Erna. I should pay her another visit sometime.'

Ernst didn't believe in the aunt at the Wolf Cemetery. He deposited the newspaper on the bench between himself and Marie, then ruffled Hasso's fur. She ran her thumbnail up and down the side seam of her skirt. The postmaster would soon be awakening from his afternoon nap, then visiting time would be over. Ernst picked up the paper again.

'It says here, the murderers' victims are to be buried tomorrow.'

'Aha.'

'At the Hörnli.'

'Aha.'

'A big ceremony. Public.'

'Hm.'

'I thought we might go.'

'Who, you and me?'

'Yes. Wouldn't you like to?'

'Why should I?'

'Just asking. You can say if you don't want to go.'

'Why shouldn't I want to go?'

'I didn't say that.'

'Or do I *have* to go?'

'I didn't say that either.'

'You think I *have* to go, just because I *once* went for a walk with them?'

'Twice, actually, but I didn't say that.'

'I don't *have* to go.'

They relapsed into silence, seated side by side with their lower lips thrust out defiantly. The lunchtime break was drawing to a close. Hasso sensed this too. He got up, yawned and stretched, then trotted over to his water bowl and had a drink. He made his way across the yard to the road, where he stared suspiciously first south, then north, and uttered a little bark. Then he returned to the bench and lay down again at Marie's feet.

'I don't *have* to go,' she said, 'but I don't see why I *shouldn't.*'

'Of course not.'

❧

'Decision of the district attorney's office, Basel City, dated

27 June 1934: Criminal proceedings against Waldemar Velte, Prussian national, born 4 August 1910, unmarried, technician, and Kurt Sandweg, Prussian national, born 3 August 1910, unmarried, metalworker, in respect of: 'First, the murders of Arnold Kaufmann, Jacques Beutter, Jakob Vollenweider, Alfred Nafzger, and Hans Maritz; secondly, the attempted murder of Walter Gohl; thirdly, the illegal use of vehicles (1 automobile and 2 bicycles), are hereby suspended owing to the death of the two accused.

'The following objects found in their room remain impounded: 1 ammunition pouch, 1 holster, 1 skeleton key, 1 pistol magazine, 1 case, 2 flashlights, 1 pocket notebook, 1 bludgeon, 14 photographs, 1 black felt hat. The following objects found on Velte's body remain impounded: 1 Walther automatic, 1 magazine containing 7 rounds, 2 ignition keys, 1 notebook. The following objects found on Sandweg's body remain impounded: 1 DRGM pistol, 1 bunch of keys comprising 3 keys and 6 ignition keys, 1 skeleton key, 1 leather wallet containing 2 car keys. The remaining articles are at the disposal of their relatives. The lady's umbrella taken into safekeeping will be returned to Fräulein Viktoria Schupp, 23 Palmenstrasse.'

Hilde Velte: 'I don't know what happened to those things. We didn't want any of them. I believe they're normally auctioned off. No, we didn't want the portable gramophone and the records either. I mean, what were we supposed to do, play them?'

The Schweizerische Kreditanstalt placed 10,000 francs at the disposal of Basel's municipal government for the dependants of Jacques Beutter, Arnold Kaufmann, Hans Maritz, Alfred Nafzger, Franz Zellweger, and Jakob Vollenweider.

❧

The following Wednesday, thousands of people converged on Hörnli Cemetery for the funeral of the three policemen who had been shot – on foot, in overcrowded buses and in long lines of private cars. Marching along in the lead came the police band, followed by 400 Basel policemen, police delegations from all over Switzerland, German custodians of the law in shakos and spiked helmets, French gendarmes in flat peaked caps, and finally the population of Basel, all keenly observed by the reporter from the *National-Zeitung.* 'Grave-faced men and women could be seen striding along, inspired by a feeling that they were in some way conveying their sympathy for the victims and their families.'

Striding along in their midst were Marie Stifter and Ernst Walder – he inspired by a feeling of ill-concealed triumph, she quivering with equally ill-concealed rage.

It was a long way to the Hörnli.

'Cold?' he asked. 'Want to go back?'

'Why should I want to go back?'

'Just asking. In case you're cold.'

'We wanted to go. Now we're going.'

The funeral service had begun by the time they reached the Hörnli. The steps leading up to the chapel were adorned with wreaths, the chapel itself was full to overflowing. Ernst took Marie's arm, elbowed his way through the throng with schoolmasterly authority, and wasn't satisfied until they were standing right in front of the coffins in the midst of senior police officers and ecclesiastical dignitaries. Then the funeral orations began: a Catholic one for Jakob Vollenweider, a Protestant one each for Hans Maritz and Alfred Nafzger, and a secular address from Police Commissioner Carl Ludwig on behalf of the Basel government.

It was a very long service.

'Still not too cold?' whispered Ernst, who had savoured his triumph to the full and would now have been prepared for a reconciliation. 'We can go home if you like.'

'Ssh!' Marie hissed. 'Why should I want to go home?'

Marie and Ernst remained in the front row to the bitter end. After a performance by the choral section of the police corps, the flag of the Police Riflemen's Association was dipped a last time in honour of the dead. Then the spokesman of the Police Federation paid tribute to the three meritorious victims, welcomed and thanked all the delegations from other forces and read out the numerous messages received. After a chorale from the police band and a communal prayer, Maritz's and Nafzger's coffins were conveyed to the crematorium while Vollenweider's was carried across to a waiting grave and committed to the earth while the police band played a musical farewell.

The crowd gradually drifted homewards. To prevent them from becoming separated, Ernst took hold of Marie's arm. In so doing he accidentally touched her breast, an inadvertence for which he apologised and she reprimanded him with a frown.

'Like to go home already?' he asked 'Or shall we go for a walk?'

'A walk? Where to?'

'The harbour. If you like. To look at the boats.'

'I've seen them, but it's a long time since I paid my aunt a visit.'

'Which aunt?'

'Aunt Erna. At the Wolf Cemetery. Mind if we visit her?'

'Why should I mind?'

'We don't have to go if you don't want to.'

'Why shouldn't I …'

And so on and so forth.

24

Life in Basel soon resumed its wonted course. True, schoolchildren continued to play 'Sandweg and Velte' in their playgrounds for months afterwards, and they all wanted to be robbers, certainly not policemen; true, the municipality made the possession of firearms subject to strict authorisation and petitioned the national government for the immediate reinforcement of frontier posts; and true, the police continued for a while to carry out stringent identity checks in the city centre – but it would be decades before any Basel policemen came under fire again.

And in other respects?

Mousy-looking bank clerk Gottfried Lindner remained loyal to the Gablenberg branch of the Stuttgarter Bank. For another 11 years he kowtowed to his late branch manager's successor, who was quite as ardent a Nazi as Feuerstein had been. In 1944 he was crushed by a collapsing concrete ceiling during a bombing raid on Stuttgart.

Waldemar Velte's brother, little Lothar of the sheath knife, got a chance to prove himself in battle shortly before the end of the war. He came home with a stomach wound that never really healed. After the war he left Germany 'to forget about the Waldemar business', as his sister Hilde put it. He spent his life working as an engineer in Iran, returned in 1966 with stomach cancer, died in 1971, and was buried in the Veltes' family plot. The graveyard is idyllically situated between a paddock and a small wood. In winter, when the trees are bare, one can see it from the Veltes' living room.

Bonnie and Clyde raided another two banks in Lancaster, Texas, and Kansas, raking in a total of $6,800. On 1 April 1934 they shot and killed two policemen on traffic duty in Grapevine, Texas, and five days later another constable in Miami, Oklahoma. They were then betrayed by Henry Methvin, the fellow gang member whom they had sprung from prison on 16 February, and who had negotiated a reduced sentence in return for his treachery. On the morning of 23 May 1934, a special task force of Texas Rangers and FBI agents was lying in wait beside a road near Arcadia, Louisiana. When the sand-coloured Ford V8 appeared at a quarter past nine, they opened fire without warning, using heavy automatic weapons. Bonnie and Clyde were hit by 167 bullets. The bullet-riddled car with the two bodies inside it was towed to the local town, where a crowd of sightseers was already waiting. It was claimed by the legal owner, a woman, who rented it out for ten dollars a week as an attraction for barbecue parties, shop openings and rodeos. Today the Ford V8 is in Whiskey Pete's Casino Hotel in Stateline, 40 miles south of Las Vegas. Also on display is a tattered, bloodstained shirt said to have been worn by Clyde Barrow on the day of his death.

Waldemar Velte's young sister Hilde suffered a great deal as a result of her brother's misdeeds. Other children pointed their fingers at her in school, her girlfriends shunned her, and clubs refused to admit her. She remained unmarried throughout her life and continued to live in her parental home, where she looked after her father and mother until they died. It came as a terrible shock to her when I tracked her down and requested an interview in writing. 'I'd hoped that the affair would have been forgotten after all this time,' she told me on the phone a few days later. Then she asked what I wanted to know, and we spoke together for a good hour.

The Basel bank clerks Haitz and Siegrist became unemployed shortly after the raid because the Wever Bank went bankrupt. Siegrist took refuge in the army recruit school, later landed a job at Basel University's library, and never went back into the banking business. Little Haitz transferred his interest from girls' legs to economics and rose to become Basel's public treasurer.

Kurt Sandweg and Waldemar Velte's graves were dug up when the cemetery was remodelled in 1959. The soil was scattered over a rectangular plot bordered by four paths, and the cemetery gardener sowed it with grass.

Willi Kollo sang *In Deine Hände* at Berlin's *Kabarett der Komiker* from 1933 onwards. Telefunken discovered the song and recorded it with the well-known tenor Marcel Wittrisch. In 1934 it could be heard issuing from every window and broadcasting station in Germany, Switzerland and Austria; and from 1936 – in the English version, which was entitled *My Heart Was Sleeping* – in the rest of Europe, Canada and the United States. Thanks to his royalties from the song, Kollo had enough to live on until after the war. He had been banned from practising his profession as a political cabarettist in January 1933, but was allowed to go on singing innocuous love songs.

Hedwig Vetter's guesthouse in Sperrstrasse was closed on public health grounds in March 1934. Unable to pay the rent without any guests, she had to move out and found herself destitute and on the streets at the age of 57. In this predicament she accepted the invitation of a former boarder of hers who had retired to a comfortable little lakeside chalet on the Titisee. She kept house for him, accepted his proposal of marriage and lived happily to a ripe old age.

The young landlady Johanna Furrer, on the other hand, voluntarily sold her guesthouse in July 1934. She travelled down the Rhine to Rotterdam by tugboat and, thanks to good fortune, charm, money and her irreproachably Aryan looks, emigrated to Vancouver on the west coast of Canada. There she opened a cake shop and became so renowned for her Swiss specialities that she had, within a few years, opened 18 branches throughout the country. She never married and lived to a ripe and healthy old age. In her latter years she resided on Vancouver Island in a comfortable old people's home on the edge of a forest containing thousand-year-old sequoias, ferns the height of a man, pumas and black bears. The balcony of her apartment afforded a view of the Pacific Ocean. At ten past two every afternoon, a pod of killer whales used to round the big rock at the northern end of the beach.

Detective Constable Walter Gohl had to spend many months in hospital before the surgeons repaired his shattered lower jaw. He left the police service and retired.

The doughty reporter from the *National-Zeitung* gradually and for no apparent reason lost interest, first in his profession and then in life in general – a misfortune that sooner or later afflicts many people who constantly view the world through a loophole. He took some civil service job or other and pretty soon drank himself to death.

Marie Stifter and Ernst Walder went to the Wolf Cemetery after the funeral. Although Marie failed to find Aunt Erna's grave, she coerced her fiancé into going for an interminable walk among the freshly turned graves, smiling triumphantly. Having got married on the third Sunday after Easter 1934, as arranged, they produced two daughters, planted numerous fruit trees and persecuted each other with unremitting animosity throughout their lives. Instead of drawing apart in the course of time, however, they moved closer together. My grandmother seldom left the house after the birth of her daughters, and my grandfather, too, spent more and more time at home after hanging up his football boots and consigning the conductor's baton, the chairmanship of the athletics club and his political offices to younger hands. Their daughters fled the poisonous atmosphere prevailing in the parental home as soon as they came of age, whereupon, in 1956, my grandfather spent 960,000 old French francs in Paris on a Citroën DS with hydropneumatic suspension – not the bottom-of-the-range model, either, but the apple-green luxury version with an aubergine sunroof and caramel leather upholstery.

The car wasn't of much practical use because every important place in the village – the schoolhouse, the bakery, the dairy, the butcher's shop, the post office, the *Zur Traube* inn – was on the doorstep. When the school holidays came, however, my grandparents packed the boot and fled from their domestic battlefield, albeit in each other's company. For the first few years they always went to Italy, venturing a bit further south every year, but later to Spain and even, after my grandfather retired, to Yugoslavia and Greece. For thousands of kilometres he sat behind the wheel with her in the passenger seat, he clicking his jaw in silence while she, with great tenacity, commented on his standard of driving. With grim determination they trudged through the Circus Maximus and the Uffizi, glided side by side along Venetian canals in gondolas, lurched up to the Acropolis on donkeyback, and rode across the Camargue on lame wild horses. Consumed with mutual hatred, they accompanied each other to bullfights, volcanic eruptions and operas. This went on until 1985, when my grandmother died of heart failure. My grandfather lived on for another ten years. When his sight began to fail he gave the Citroën DS to my mother, who passed it on to me, and I pretty soon wrecked the car because I hadn't the money to maintain it. My grandfather continued to tend his apple orchard, sinking steadily deeper into a slough of bitterness and loneliness from which neither his daughters nor his grandchildren could ever redeem him.

The birth of the Citroën DS in 1955 was, incidentally, a revolutionary event in automotive history. With four cylinders and an engine capacity of two litres, it attained 74 horsepower at 4500 revolutions per minute, had disk brakes on all four wheels and bodywork of timeless elegance and beauty. Thanks to its front-wheel drive, hydropneumatic suspension and power steering, it won numerous races after overcoming a few teething troubles, for instance the two-litre class of the Monte Carlo Rally in 1959, the Adria Rally, the Wiking Rally, the Acropolis Rally, the Coupe des Alpes, the Liège-Rome-Liège, and the German Rally.

Dorly Schupp had a hard time of it after the dramatic events in Margarethen Park. Stones came hurtling through her bedroom window three times in the succeeding ten nights. Anonymous poison pen letters lurked in her mailbox every morning, and people stared at her in the record department during the day.

'To the police of the city of Basel! Sandweg and Velte's lady friend – that worthy girl and ally of Sandweg and Velte, the one who shared their implicit trust and has displayed such contradictory behaviour, did not deliberately help to get her friends tracked down. She obeyed the dictates of the moment. She knew that no harm would come to her in the park, because the pair were counting on her previous loyalty and complicity. No, that worthy girl is not to blame for falling into the criminals' arms on first acquaintance, but she obediently and calculatingly accompanied them in their intrigues from guesthouse to guesthouse and lived on a share of her faithful friends' blood-spattered money. Her conduct is precisely that of a person complicit in their criminal activities; she no doubt would gladly have kept out of it, and at the last moment she pretended to be uninvolved. Police, are you so sold on the praises that have been heaped on that 'worthy girl' that you don't dare lay a finger on this suspicious running sore for fear of looking foolish? If the police won't take note, others will do so for them. Signed, a friend.'

❧

The *National-Zeitung* came to Dorly Schupp's defence: 'From motives of confused romanticism, certain people, notably women, claim that she should not have gone into the park to betray her "friends". Things are different in the cinema, admittedly, but let us recall the case in point. The woman had not become friends with Velte and Sandweg because she more or less regarded them as Robin Hoods to whom one should be loyal unto death, through thick and thin. No, she believed, justifiably and in good faith, that she was dealing with two decent, well-brought-up, well-educated young men. When bereft of this illusion, which hit her hard, there was only one thing she could do: assist our authorities in capturing those monsters to the best of her ability.'

Dorly Schupp continued to live with her mother and occupy her girlhood room at 23 Palmenstrasse. She rose over the years to become senior assistant in the record department at Globus. Her trail peters out on 23 December 1942, two months after her mother died of a heart attack while hanging up some washing. According to information from the residents' registration bureau in Basel, that was when Viktoria Schupp moved to 72 Route de Rhône, Geneva. However, no person of that name has ever been registered as living there.

The End

ALEX CAPUS was born in 1961 in Normandy. He has published numerous works, including novels, collections of short stories and essays, as well as translations into German of *A Confederacy of Dunces* by John Kennedy Toole and three novels by the American writer John Fante. His works to have been published in English translation include *A Matter of Time*, *Léon and Louise* and the travelogue *Sailing by Starlight: In Search of Treasure Island*. Alex Capus lives with his wife and five sons in Olten, Switzerland.

ALSO BY ALEX CAPUS

LÉON AND LOUISE

Fiction, Literature | 9781908323-13-2

A MATTER OF TIME

Fiction, Literature | 9781907822-03-2

SAILING BY STARLIGHT

IN SEARCH OF TREASURE ISLAND AND ROBERT LOUIS STEVENSON

Travelogue | 9781907973-74-1